"The heart knows things the mind..."

SYSTEMA PARADOXA

ACCOUNTS OF CRYPTOZOOLOGICAL IMPORT

VOLUME 22
MOTHER'S INSTINCT
A TALE OF THE DOBHAR-CHÚ

AS ACCOUNTED BY SHERRI COOK WOOSLEY

NEOPARADOXA
Pennsville, NJ
2024

PUBLISHED BY
NeoParadoxa
A division of eSpec Books
PO Box 242
Pennsville, NJ 08070
www.especbooks.com

Copyright © 2024 Sherri Cook Woosley

ISBN: 978-1-956463-63-7
ISBN (ebook): 978-1-956463-62-0

All rights reserved. No part of the contents of this book may be reproduced or transmitted in any form or by any means without the written permission of the publisher.

All persons, places, and events in this book are fictitious and any resemblance to actual persons, places, or events is purely coincidental.

Interior Design: Danielle McPhail
www.sidhenadaire.com

Cover Art: Jason Whitley
Cover Design: Mike and Danielle McPhail, McP Digital Graphics
Interior Illustration: Jason Whitley

Copyediting: Greg Schauer and John L. French

Dedication

To Jules, Al, and Jay

Hope your book club enjoys this.

Chapter One

Seatbelts off, car parked, and doors unlocked in case of a water emergency. Nervous, Rosie couldn't help triple-checking that she'd followed the captain's instructions. Next stop: Glenade Island, Ireland. The ferry's horn blasted into the evening and then the rocking started as it launched away from the mainland. In her car, Rosie tensed her hands on the steering wheel, even though she had no control over the boat. This was the last leg of a journey that had started many, many hours ago on the other side of the Atlantic Ocean. The flight from Baltimore to Dublin had been long but not difficult. Then she'd had to get the rental car and drive northwest out of the city and through never-ending green hills of fluffy sheep and stony ruins of ancient walls. Picturesque? Yes. Could she appreciate it? Not yet. Exhaustion teased at Rosie's focus and all she could think about was crawling into a warm bed and sleeping. As it was, her eyes burned, she was jittery from bad airline coffee, and she desperately needed to pee, but hadn't wanted the ferry to leave without her. This was the last trip to the island today. So she'd ignored the toilets and driven onto the ferry right behind the van carrying the other graduate students. She was close to finishing her Ph.D. after two years of teaching ninth grade Social Studies during the day and then taking graduate classes at night. This opportunity — a semester abroad to study Celtic mythology in Ireland — was too important to mess up. She needed firsthand research and local knowledge to finish her degree. Maybe even gain the notice of the academic community. It didn't hurt that this location was the least expensive travel option. Most other students were probably turned off because the island was isolated, but that would be perfect for Rosie. She just wanted peace and quiet.

Looking at the mainland in the rearview mirror, Rosie saw the roundabout they'd taken to get to the ferry. To the left of the roundabout, a towering pile of overturned dirt made yellow construction equipment look like toys abandoned for the day. Metal caution fences marked the edge. An artist's drawing of whatever was being built sat next to the fence, but Rosie couldn't make it out from this far away.

Stop looking over your shoulder, she chided herself. No one is following. The island is small and private. Safe.

"Are we there yet?" The question, asked by every child on every journey ever, drifted from the backseat.

"I sincerely hope so," Rosie answered.

"Because I need to pee."

"Same."

A long-suffering sigh from the backseat made Rosie grin. Dally had been a trooper on this trip, or as much of a trooper as one could expect from a six-year-old. The special trip bag had worked well. Rosie had packed and labeled individual snacks, a plastic loom with colorful rubber bands to make bracelets, earbuds for an audiobook, crayons, and two new coloring books, one with cartoon dog characters and one with animal mothers and babies in their natural habitats.

"This ferry is taking us the last bit from the tip of County Leitrim to Glenade Island." Rosie licked her chapped lips. "Today you've been on a plane and inside a car that's riding on a boat. What do you think?"

"I don't want to be in a plane or a car or a boat."

"I know, sweetie. I was just teasing. Once the ferry docks, we'll be there." She looked in the rearview mirror again, but this time the view was blurred by grey.

Frowning, Rosie rolled down her car window and thrust her hand into the cold, clammy air. Where had the fog come from? It seemed to move between the cars in encircling rings so that the farthest vehicles were simply gone. The van with graduate students was still visible, but it too was being swallowed as the fog writhed. The guidebook had said that weather in Ireland changed quickly, especially on the coast, but this was unsettling.

Concern made her blink repeatedly as if she could make the fog disappear. She was isolated from the rest of the ferry. Or maybe they weren't on the ferry anymore. Maybe they'd left one world and entered another. Just like the Irish stories that Rosie had read in the safety of her living room. Maybe they were in the Irish Otherworld of supernatural gods and goddesses. Or had wandered into one of the stories that ended with humans entering the world of Faerie and disappearing for one hundred years.

"Mom! I don't like this."

You're a mother, Rosie scolded herself, *keep your imagination in check.* An imagination that she'd obviously passed along to Dahlia. One of them had to be practical.

"Don't worry, honey. This is just a big cloud that we're sailing through. Very common for summertime on an island." She had no idea if that was true, but it sounded plausible. And experiencing this cloud helped her understand why fog played such a big role in the mythology of this region. Ha! She was already learning something just from physically being here.

"I'll be right back, Dahlia. I want to see if the island is visible yet."

Rosie got out of the car. Immediately, the fog stuck to her skin and soaked into her clothes. The ferry's foghorn sent a loud blast into the air, but the sound was absorbed by the surrounding greyness. Her senses screamed that she was all alone because she couldn't see anything more than a foot away in any direction, including the sky. Everything else was gone. Rosie made her way to the railing, tripping over a thick coil of rope. Panic set in. Maybe this was too much, maybe she'd been too ambitious to come here as a single parent and non-traditional student. Rosie liked the idea of Indiana Jones—the adventurous archeologist with a penchant for occult objects—but had to admit she was more of an armchair librarian.

She'd applied for this special research class months ago by submitting her letter of interest with a personal essay about how being on location in Ireland would provide a unique opportunity to explore the role of women in Celtic mythology. Rosie had argued that while she could bring literary analysis to the characters of Rhiannon from *The Mabinogi* and Medb from *The Tain*, she needed time in this country to understand the older layers of these medieval texts. Basically, she needed a chance to understand the forces that she didn't even know she didn't know. While the rejection hadn't been surprising, it had still hurt. Studying comparative folklore and mythology was part of remembering what she'd loved before her marriage and the nightmare that followed. Clicking 'submit' on the application had felt so brave. The rejection had felt... deserved. The administration had known that she wasn't good enough.

Then, two weeks ago, the phone call came. She'd made it off the waitlist. A quick turnaround with her school's final grades, advance rent to the apartment's landlord, and she booked the flights.

Rosie gripped the railing until her fingers ached and searched the fog. She could hear the water beneath so that's where she focused. There was a gap between the water and the fog and Rosie's shoulders relaxed just a little. Then, from the water, a head emerged. Black beady eyes met Rosie's. Dark fur slicked back around its head and long whiskers quivered. The creature made a high-pitched whistling sound and then sank back into the water. The encounter took only a brief second. Rosie's brows drew together as she tried to figure out what she'd seen. Her first thought had been a dog, but what was a dog doing this far out from the mainland? A seal? An otter? She searched the water again, but nothing moved.

Soon the fog began to dissipate and lights from the island ahead came into view. On the map the island was small—only a dot—but in person the limestone jutted from the sea in a breathtaking view. The village nestled in the cove, but behind it the rest of the island climbed upward into a cliff overlooking the ocean. Even in the evening light, the brilliant green of the island played against the topaz sky. Then the ferry's horn sounded again and Rosie hurried back to her car. A moment later she followed the school van off the ferry and onto the primary road of the island, stopping about halfway down. This was the only village on the small island so most of the permanent shops were in a tidy row with a market area with stalls for vendors marked off closer to the dock.

"We're here," Rosie said, trying to be cheerful. It was 9:30 at night and the sun had just set, causing the remaining light to create curious shapes and shadows of the buildings and surrounding landscape. They'd parked in front of the only building with lights and people. Neon lighting proclaimed: Sea Monster's Sauce. Just in case the name didn't give away what the sauce was, the huge sign announcing GUINNESS with a picture of a pint glass was there to help.

Rosie helped Dally out of the car seat. The little girl's brown hair, a lighter shade than Rosie's chestnut color, had come out of its pony tail and Cheerios spilled from her lap. Oh well. There'd be time to clean up the car later. Right now, the van driver was unloading luggage so this would be a good time for a bathroom break. Holding Dally's hand,

Rosie pushed open the door to the crowded pub. A quartet played music in the corner while the audience clapped along. Later, it would be fun to check out. For now, it was a challenge. At 5'4" and towing a child, Rosie had to press against the wall as she weaved through the crowd muttering versions of 'sorry' and 'excuse me' until she found the hallway in the back with the bathroom.

Once they were back outside, Rosie glanced around in disbelief. The van was gone and the ferry had pulled away from the dock. Seeing three people carrying suitcases and wearing backpacks about to enter the building next to the pub, she sprinted after them.

"Hey," she called. "Where did the van go? Did the driver hand out room keys?"

The group turned around and Rosie had to force herself not to be defensive. She was a single mom much older than these three. That didn't mean they couldn't all get along.

"Oh. We didn't know where you went." The young woman who spoke appeared to be in her early 20's with straight blonde hair, tanned skin, and wearing a name-brand athletic clothing line that cost more than Rosie could afford. "I'm Peyton and this is Erika." She pointed to another young woman who could have been related to Peyton except where the former had cooler toned highlights, the latter had warmer toned highlights in her blonde hair. "We found out we're both hospitality majors so that's really lucky."

Rosie did not ask why that was lucky. Instead, she shook the hand that was being offered by a young man with olive skin and dark hair gelled back. His shirt had two buttons undone to reveal a gold chain and his sleeves rolled to reveal a matching gold watch. "Dimitri. Business major. I'm here to prove to my parents that they should let me run part of the family business." He winked.

"Ah," Rosie said, unsure if she was supposed to ask what the family business was or laugh at the mafia reference. "Nice to meet you. I'm Rosie, this is my daughter Dahlia, and I'm here to research Celtic mythology."

"Celtic?" Peyton made a face. "Like it starts with a 'K'? I thought it was like an 'S' like the Boston team."

"Nope, definitely not," Rosie said, keeping her smile anchored. "The Celts are an Iron Age people who originated in the middle of Europe and there are six regions that still have their own language and rituals so it's fascinating to compare—"

"Uh. That does sounds fascinating," Erika interrupted, "but we've been traveling all day and want to go to bed."

"No, of course. I traveled all day too." Rosie's face burned. "Is this the way to the rooms? When are we supposed to go on the field trips?"

Erika sighed. "We went over all this like five minutes ago."

"Sorry." Rosie swallowed. "I needed to use the restroom."

"Boring!" Dimitri grinned. "We thought you went in to get a pint. Ready to get this trip started."

With her six-year-old daughter? Yeah, that made a lot of sense.

"We already kind of buddied up in the van so it made sense for us to be a group. And we chose the more modern option." Peyton shrugged her shoulders. "The other room is across the street. See the spiral staircase?"

Dally pulled on Rosie's hand. She was so tired. They all were. This was not the time for a fight. Rosie gritted her teeth. "Sure. I see it."

"Cool," Peyton said, turning back to the door. "We have key cards, but he said your key is in the door."

"Sounds very secure."

"Get the Wi-Fi code and everything from the bookstore lady underneath your room."

"Right."

Peyton swiped her card over the lock. When it turned green, she pulled open the door and then walked inside, wheeling her giant pink suitcase behind. Erika and Dimitri followed.

"Were you going to tell me any of this if I hadn't chased you down?" Rosie called.

Through the window she saw the group standing in front of an elevator. Peyton said something and they all laughed. Was it paranoid to think it was about her?

"Who cares?" she whispered, answering her question.

"Mommy?" Dally pulled on her hand again. "Please. Can we go to bed?"

"Of course."

Rosie went to their rental car and popped the trunk. She looked at her suitcase and then the outside spiral staircase. Nope. No way she could lug the suitcase up step by step. But what other option was there? A crane on the roof? Maybe a crane like the bird? It could be a new myth. The bird would fly the Americans' suitcase up and then she'd have to do a favor for the bird. Maybe he would turn back into a prince, and he'd give her a financial reward so that she could pay off student loans.

"Will you carry me?" Dalhia looked up, her pale face pinched with exhaustion, her lower lip trembling as she tried to hold back tears.

"Aww, kitten. We've pushed too hard today, haven't we?" Rosie shook her head. Figuring out how to get suitcases up the stairs was a problem for the morning. She shrugged into her bookbag and Dally already wore hers. A click to lock the car and then Rosie scooped up her daughter.

With one hand on the banister for balance and the other hand pressed against Dally's back, Rosie mounted the staircase. Her daughter's head rested on Rosie's shoulder and each soft snore gave her the strength to climb one more stair in what seemed a never-ending spiral. Finally, though, they reached the landing. A faint glow came from inside and it was enough to see that, indeed, a key waited in the lock. Adjusting her stance, Rosie reached out to turn the key. The door opened with a squeal of hinges that did not wake Dally. Two bunkbeds. They already had sheets on. Good enough.

Gently unwrapping Dally's arms, Rosie lowered her daughter onto the bed. Dally took after her father's build, with long arms and legs. Her coloring — the light brown hair, blue eyes, and pale skin — was also like her Swiss-American father rather than Rosie's Ukrainian Jewish heritage. But Dally's personality was more like Rosie's: an introvert who loved books and animals. Rosie shook out the quilt folded at the bottom of the bed and covered her daughter. Then Rosie locked the door, placed the key on the table, and fell into the other bed.

Chapter Two

When Rosie blinked her eyes open, she had no idea what time it was. Her vision was blurry—probably from either allergies or dry eyes from traveling on the airplane. She glanced at the other bed and saw the lumpy quilt. Good. Dally was still sleeping. Rosie let out a big sigh and then sat up, propping the pillow against the headboard.

Last night had been rushed but now she could examine the room that would be theirs for the next four weeks. An angled window between the bunk beds let in a patch of sunlight to light the circular rug on the floor. The rug was a rich red, patterned with cats dressed in hunt jackets riding horses. Beyond the rug, a wooden table with three chairs pushed against the opposite wall, and to the right, across from the outer door, was an open hallway that led to what, she guessed, was a bathroom.

Tiptoeing so she could enjoy a few moments of alone time, Rosie picked up her bookbag and went to the hallway. Two rooms opened to the left and a closed door ended the hallway. Rosie went to that door and turned the handle, but it was locked. Probably the owner's suite. The room closest to the locked door was a tiny kitchen. A stove with a tea kettle sat next to a cabinet filled with dishes. The drawers underneath held basic cooking pots and pans. There was barely space to turn around, but against the other wall was a washing machine and a folded drying rack leaned against the wall under a framed picture of a castle. Rosie pulled back filmy curtains from a window. Ah, the spiral staircase was on Main Street, but this view was the opposite side. A wild meadow full of tall grass and colorful flowers swayed in the wind. Several cottages with thatched roofs sat on a rugged road off to the left. In the distance, beyond the flower meadow, it looked like a creek cut a path through an embankment in front of a forest of old-growth trees.

Rosie wondered if that was an inlet from the Atlantic or whether there was a freshwater source on the island.

Movement caught Rosie's attention and she sucked in a breath as she realized there a buck in the meadow. He'd lifted his head in alarm, exposing a flash of white hair at his throat. He couldn't be that old because his antlers were small with two tines each, branching to the sky. He pawed the ground and then lowered his head to the tall grass again.

Dally would love to see this. What a perfect start to their first day in Ireland. Rosie hurried to the bunk bed and shook the quilt. Even as her mind registered that her hand was sinking down instead of meeting a warm little body, Rosie's instincts kicked in. She yanked the covers back to reveal an empty bed. Then she snatched up the pillow and threw it to the foot of the bed. Of course it made no sense that Dally would be hiding under the pillow, but it also didn't make sense that her daughter wasn't here.

"Dally? Dahlia Harper Connell!" Rosie touched each section of the bunk beds and then leaned against the table. Her mind registered that something was missing. Her gaze jerked to the door. The key sat in the lock.

Rosie flew down the spiral staircase — it wasn't nearly as imposing during the day — and looked up and down Main Street, desperate for a clue as to where her daughter had gone. Last night the street had been quiet, but the ferry must have come this morning because an open-air market was doing a brisk business by the dock. Beyond the shops in the other direction were stone buildings that looked like a church and school. So many places a child could decide to explore, but Dally didn't have a cell phone or any way to be tracked. Rosie strained to hear a child's voice calling out from the chaos of people talking and doors slamming. What if Kenny had found them? What if—

A sudden rapping on the window behind Rosie made her jump. She pivoted to face the bookstore and there, standing inside the display, was Dally. Rosie leaned against the window, palms pressed to the glass, in disbelief. Dally wore the extra outfit from the carry-on and an enormous grin. Dropping her hands, Rosie took a step back — both physically and mentally. Control, she told herself. Dally is all right; her father had not kidnapped her. In fact, Dally was standing inside a giant cat playground and looked ecstatic. Gilt letters on a maroon frame proclaimed: *Saoirse's*. Smaller gilt letters elaborated: Bookstore, Cat Café, and Flower Mart.

Rosie pulled open the door and a little bell jangled. Stepping inside, she stood in a foyer of dark wood next to a table decorated with what looked like matching vintage stained-glass lamps. The shop had been converted from a house. Stairs were straight ahead. That was probably the owner's apartment on the other side of the locked door. When Rosie leaned to the right, she could see bookcases while the scent of cinnamon and warm fruit wafted from the café section to the left. The most important part, though, was the narrow door that blended into the foyer. It opened and Dally popped out.

"Mom!" She rushed forward and hugged Rosie's legs. "You slept forever."

The hug brought instant relief. Rosie knelt so she could look Dahlia in the face. She had expressive blue eyes that showed every hurt and every joy. "Sweetie, you scared me this morning because I didn't know where you were."

"I waited a long time for you." Dahlia let her arms drop down, her hand catching at the cloth on her shirt.

"We have rules here just like back home. You know you're not allowed to wander around without me."

"But I didn't." Dahlia rubbed the shirt between her thumb and index finger, a nervous habit. "This is part of our house. The downstairs. I stayed right here and played with the kitties."

Rosie nodded, understanding the logic. "This part of the building is a store. The part upstairs with the beds is our special area. Do you understand?"

Dally nodded.

"Well then," a male voice spoke with an Irish lilt, "you must be little Dahlia's mother."

Rosie, still kneeling, looked up and up. The man had to be at least six feet tall—did they use meters here?—with a sturdy build complimented by a dark sweater and worn jeans. His hair was sandy brown and rumpled like he'd come in from a windy day at the beach. It was also long enough that he had to keep sweeping it away from his green eyes. He looked the very image of an Irishman, including a slightly crooked nose that suggested it had been broken.

She scrambled to her feet.

"She's kept us very entertained this morning, haven't you, darlin'?"

Dally stared at the man and nodded.

"Do you want to take your mother in and show her breakfast?"

Dally nodded again. She took Rosie's hand and pulled her toward the café. The man followed behind.

The café held the typical clusters of tables and chairs, but the part that drew Rosie's attention was the counter along the front that shared a window with the cat playground. It would be a perfect place to work because she could watch both the cats and the island routine without feeling like she was on display. Flowers, probably from the meadow behind the store, filled the vases on the tables with a riot of colors: pink and white, yellow, and bright red. The most delicious smell, though, came from the back. A full espresso bar with a bean grinder took up half the space and a towering display case full of various pastries took up the other. Next to the pastry display was a refrigerated shelf with yogurt, cheeses, deli meats, and bowls of mixed fruit. In the middle part of the counter, next to the cash register, sat a black cauldron labeled 'Steel Cut Oatmeal.' Toppings—everything from brown sugar to raisins to slivered almonds—were organized next to it in tidy pots with miniature spoons.

"Not too shabby, is it now?" He had a flirty half-smile as he made a point of gesturing the entire length of the display.

"No," Rosie said, flustered at the handsome man's attention. "It looks good."

"It's past time for breakfast, Dylan O'Maver, so I'll thank you to stop offering what isn't yours."

Rosie gulped as she turned to face the annoyed woman, abruptly aware she was still wearing her pajamas: rumpled t-shirt featuring a crow tangled in red yarn and sweats with a jelly stain.

In contrast, the woman personified sophisticated elegance with glossy black hair cut in an angle to her chin. Her skin was milk white and she had an oval face with grey eyes surrounded by long sweeping lashes. She wore both a disdainful expression and white linen pants with a sleeveless shirt that showed off long limbs intended for languishing. She flowed instead of walked across the room as if it wasn't worth the bother. Rosie had the impression that she'd seen this woman on the cover of some magazine or another but couldn't place it.

"Now, Jordan, what kind of host would you be if you didn't offer your American guest a decent breakfast on her very first day here?"

"Maybe you should worry about running your pub instead of trying to run my café." Jordan stepped behind the counter and took in Rosie. "You are Anne-Rose Connell?"

"Yes. That's me, but my friends call me Rosie."

"The registration packet said Anne-Rose."

Were they having an argument about her name? Rosie shook her head. "I don't generally have breakfast so there's no problem."

"A continental breakfast is included with your registration," Dylan said. "Please help yourself if you're hungry."

"It's available weekdays from 8-10AM," Jordan said tartly.

"We want our guests happy," Dylan said through clenched teeth. "So that we get more guests. See how that works?"

Jordan lifted a shoulder like she was shutting Dylan and his opinions out of the conversation. "Your daughter had a bowl of oatmeal and a hot chocolate."

"You gave Dally food without checking with me?" Rosie blinked. Sure, this place was more informal than the US, but you couldn't even bring in homecooked desserts to school. Parents had to send in storebought with an ingredient list. "What if she'd had allergies?"

Jordan tilted her head and called out to Dahlia. "Do you have any food allergies?"

"No." Dally shook her head.

"Doesn't seem that complicated." Jordan looked back at Rosie. "And you weren't around. Better that I starve the child?"

"I'm her mother—"

"Clearly—"

"And I'd appreciate if you would check with me first."

The two women stared at each other: Rosie with flushed cheeks and clenched fists and Jordan posing with a hand on her hip and a bored expression.

"The oatmeal was really good," Dally whispered into the silence.

"Of course it was, darlin'," and then you went and played with the cats all the morning, nice as you could be," Dylan said, overly jovial. "Did you want to introduce your mom? Start with Irish Teddy. He's the nicest."

"I like Esmerelda, too." Dahlia reached for Rosie's hand. "Come on, I want to show you the secret door."

They went back to the foyer and the narrow door that closed flush against the dark wood. Rosie followed Dahlia through and had to admit that it was whimsical. They were in a glass box sandwiched between Main Street and the café, but it felt cozy because of the way the platforms had been built like tree houses connected by bridges. One house was a flower with giant petals as perches. Another of the houses looked like a mushroom and the red top was a scratch pad. Toys were tucked here and there like a game of Hide and Go Seek and bits of catnip showed that some of the balls held extra treats. A cat door in the corner allowed access to and from the café.

"Teddy? *Pssst.* Irish Teddy." Dahlia checked the cat apartments until she squealed. "There you are!"

Gently cradling a cat, Dahlia turned around and presented a very large black cat with a white handkerchief-shape on his chest and white splotch across his nose. "Ms. Jordan says he's a Tuxedo."

Rosie scratched behind his ears. Teddy rumbled with contentment, the vibration a motor.

"He's adorable," Rosie said, captivated.

"Esmerelda is all black, but teeny-tiny. Ms. Jordan says she's probably going to be a witch's familiar when she grows up."

"Well, Ms. Jordan is certainly up on her folklore," Rosie said, half hoping the elegant woman would overhear.

From outside the window raised voices became audible. Dahlia was hunting for Esmerelda, but Rosie stepped to the glass to look out. Three men were shouting in front of Ernie's Fish and Tackle a few shops down.

One man, clothes wet, waved his arms angrily.

The bookstore bell tinkled as Jordan and Dylan went out to join the men. Then the Hotel twins—Peyton and Erika—appeared from the post office, also attracted by the noise.

Curious, Rosie said, "Stay here, Dally. I'll be right back." She hurried outside.

The angry man, aware of the gathering crowd, struggled to calm down. "You," he said, pointing at the man wearing a cap that had 'Ernie' written in cursive, "took my money and then sent me out to be attacked."

Rosie sidled up to Dylan and looked up at him questioningly. Dylan kept his eyes on the men, but leaned down and whispered, "These two tourists rented a fishing boat from Ernie this morning. Says they were attacked by something long and brown in the water. Big enough to swim under the kayak and flip them over. They got out of the water with their fishing gear, but they left the kayak because they're scared to go back for it. Ernie says they owe him either a kayak or the money to replace it."

"Ah," Rosie said. "Do things like this happen often in Ireland?"

Dylan glanced down at her, eyes crinkling as he smiled. "This is a land of stories and magic. What else would you expect?"

"But did the mysterious 'thing' bite you?" Jordan called out in a bored voice. "Are you bleeding?"

"No, I'm not bleeding." The angry tourist's face flushed so red Rosie worried he was going to have a stroke. "Do I have to have proof of a missing limb to be taken seriously on this damned island?"

Jordan shrugged a perfect shoulder. "Merely curious."

Ernie, meanwhile, shook his finger at the angry man. "There's no mystery creature out there. And if you keep saying it then all the tourists are going to refuse to rent from me. Summer is when I make my money for the year. So just admit you were drunk and fell out of the boat and didn't feel like bringing it back."

"Or what?" The angry man demanded. "Because I won't be lying."

"Sounds like you already are." The men were nose to nose now, and the other tourist was pulling back on the angry man's arm.

Rosie leaned closer to Dylan and whispered, "I thought that I was going to be studying ancient myths, not current ones."

"Aw, this is a fish story, not a fairy tale." Dylan stepped forward between Ernie and the tourist and raised his voice. "Alright, now. Let's come and have a pint on the house. You can tell your story from the beginning to all these curious people. They'll have to buy their own, of course. Ernie, why don't you go get the kayak and show the island that there's nothing to be scared of." Dylan laughed good-naturedly as he took each tourist's arm and propelled them toward the pub. Sure enough, the rest of the crowd followed, except the bookstore owner.

"Idiots," Jordan said without rancor. "They're all idiots." She pivoted and went back toward her bookstore.

"Wait a second," Rosie called. "I have to bring two suitcases inside—is there another way besides the outside stairs?"

"Well, Anne-Rose," Jordan said, pushing her shiny hair behind one ear, "I suppose you can bring them in through the main door. There's an elevator. I'll unlock the upstairs door for you."

"Thank you, I appreciate that," Rosie said, careful to be courteous. "But please call me Rosie."

"You said that was for your friends." Jordan raised an eyebrow. "We're not friends."

Chapter Three

First item on the agenda: sightseeing. Rosie and Dally walked the length of Main Street and window-shopped at the craft supply store, received a free "brown roll" at the grocery store, examined the postcards in front of the post office, and were very impressed by the store at the end selling handmade blankets and quilts from local artists. Then, getting tired, they stopped across the street from the blanket shop at a small bakery to get tea and a treat.

The woman in the bakery—Mrs. Troutskill—gave Dally a cookie with raspberry compote in the middle. It would have been a normal interaction except that half an hour earlier they'd seen Mrs. Troutskill in the grocery store placing fresh baked bread loaves on the shelves.

The woman had white hair and watery blue eyes behind a pair of glasses, hands with swollen joints and a cute dress with sensible shoes that, Rosie guessed, offered arch support. Yes, it was the same woman.

"Thank you," Dally said politely as she accepted the cookie. "I liked the roll you gave me too."

The woman chuckled. "Oh no, dear, I'm the Bakery Mrs. Troutskill. I make the cakes and pies, custards and tarts. And cookies. I make so many types of cookies that I've forgotten how many recipes I know. Each day I wake up and just see what I remember." She chuckled again. "And what's your name, little sweetling?"

"My name is still Dahlia." Dally looked at Rosie for help, but Rosie was just as lost. "You asked me that before."

"The Grocery Mrs. Troutskill asked you," the woman said slowly, as if explaining something important.

"And we met the Grocery Mrs. Troutskill?" Rosie asked, feeling like this was a game where she didn't know the rules. "Who bakes bread?"

"All kinds of bread," Mrs. Troutskill said, pleased that they finally understood. "I prefer the sourdough with a bit of soft sheep cheese to go with my morning tea. I'm just like a hobbit who likes to have second breakfast." As if this had reminded her, Mrs. Troutskill said, "And would you each care for a cup of tea? Cream and sugar?"

"Yes, please," Rosie said. "Dally would like a lemon or orange tea and I'll take a cup of—"

"Well now, dearie, that's not really a tea, is it? All those flowers and herbs floating around. That's a tisane."

"May she have it?" Rosie asked, beginning to regret the impulse to stop for a snack.

"Certainly. The child would like a tisane. And what would you like?"

"A slice of iced pound cake?" Rosie smoothed her eyebrow to buy time. "Ah. Maybe you can just recommend one of the teas."

"No need to be embarrassed. You're a Yankee, aren't you? I can tell by your accent. I'll make you a cup of Darjeeling." Mrs. Troutskill turned away to select two fancy cups and saucers from a shelf. After setting them down and putting the water kettle on to heat, the woman turned back around and seemed surprised to see them still standing at the counter. "Sit down at the table and I'll bring it to you, won't I? There's no rush."

Bemused, Rosie nodded. In America there was a sense of urgency—you go to a restaurant and eat quickly so that the next party can come in. That way the server had the most opportunity to make tips. Apparently, it was different here… whether that meant Ireland or this particular island, Rosie didn't know yet.

There were only two tables in the shop. Dally chose the circular one in the corner beside a large plant. At first Rosie wondered how there could be enough business to sustain the shop on this small island, but soon Jordan came in. The bell over the door jangled.

"Good afternoon, Mrs. Troutskill. Regular order for the pastry case tomorrow morning."

"Of course, dearie." The woman punched numbers into an ancient cash register. "Maybe I'll bring Hot Milk Cake over. Is that the one Irish Teddy likes?"

"He certainly seems to."

Leaving, Jordan nodded toward their table, managing to not actually meet Rosie's eyes. Why was the woman so unfriendly? It was nothing explicit, but Rosie could feel it.

Impulsively, Rosie called out, "We're going for a walk to the cliffs."

Jordan's hand gripped the door handle, but she took the time to actually look at Rosie, so she felt like she'd won.

"Good views from there. Make sure not to fall off." Jordan pushed the door open and disappeared.

Rosie deflated. The people on this island were characters. Ernie the fisherman arguing with the tourist. Dylan the smooth-talking charmer of a barkeep, the mystery of Grocery vs. Bakery Mrs. Troutskill. But it was Jordan's coolness that bothered her the most.

"Afternoon." Another young woman walked in with a toddler on her hip. "Mama needs a birthday cake for next weekend."

"That's fine." Mrs. Troutskill wiped her hands on her apron. "She'll be wanting it for the Midsummer *ceili*?"

"That's right."

"Hopefully the weather will hold."

"If it doesn't, you just have to wait five minutes and it'll be different."

Money exchanged hands and the woman left. Then the kettle started whistling. Mrs. Troutskill poured steaming water into the cups.

"I'm not going to set the timer, mind." Mrs. Troutskill tapped her forehead and winked at Dally. "I've got it up here."

A door slammed from the back of the bakery and Mrs. Troutskill took two more cups down, deftly measuring loose tea into strainers and sliding two muffins onto plates.

Humming, she then loaded their tea cups onto a tray and added a plate with a generous slice of pound cake. The tray wobbled a bit as she brought it over and Rosie pushed back her chair to help, but the tray landed on the table in one piece.

"Enjoy your tisane and tea and cake," Mrs. Troutskill said. "It's quite nice to have visitors on the island."

Then, from the back of the store, another Mrs. Troutskill appeared. Together the small differences became apparent. They were not, after all, wearing the same dress. It was the same style that had thrown Rosie off. And Grocery Mrs. Troutskill had a pink ribbon in her hair while Bakery Mrs. Troutskill had a chain attached to her glasses.

Dally jumped up from the table and pressed against the counter. "You're twins!"

The older women looked at each other and smiled. One picked up the plates with muffins and the other picked up the cups of tea. In concert, they moved toward the open table for what was clearly an afternoon ritual.

"One mystery solved." Rosie said.

Grocery Mrs. Troutskill looked at her, eyes twinkling, and said, "Don't worry, dearie, this island has plenty more."

Dally had followed the sisters to their table. "But why do you have the same names?"

Bakery Mrs. Troutskill smiled. "We married brothers. They weren't twins, but they were very nice while they lasted."

Grocery Mrs. Troutskill sighed. "It would have been better if they'd been twins."

From Main Street Rosie and Dahlia followed the dirt road up into the hills and passed a series of stone walls and small farms. The land had probably belonged to the same families for centuries. Some had cows wearing bells out front and others had goats. She was so lucky to be able to see how the island inhabitants were maintaining their unique way of life. There would be plenty of new material to bring to the myths and legends she was analyzing.

Finally, they came to the end of the dirt road and looked out over the Atlantic Ocean crashing against the cliff. The top itself was layers of jagged rock softened by the green moss and lichen growing along the layers. Wind whipped her clothes and hair. Below, the water was a blue-green with a frothy white. It was all so beautiful that Rosie could imagine she stood in a photograph, except that she could smell the salty air and hear the cries of birds as they circled near their nests on the cliff. It suddenly reminded Rosie of the ride over on the ferry and the creature she'd glimpsed with the slick, wet head and the beady black eyes.

"It's like we can see forever," Dally said. She sighed happily. "Because we're so high up."

"Yup. This island was formed by a volcano a long time ago. The magma built up and broke the ocean's surface." Rosie mimed an explosion with her hands. "The island is higher on this side, facing the ocean, while the town is on the lower section that is closest to Ireland. After this island formed, it was colonized by plants and animals, but there's still a bunch of hardened magma underneath the water that we can't see."

Dally took a step closer to the cliff face and Rosie had to press her lips together not to issue a warning. Generally, Dahlia wasn't a reckless child; instead, she tended to be cautious. Therefore, Rosie wanted to make sure she didn't squash any adventurous instincts.

"Are caves down there? Maybe under the water?"

Rosie shrugged. "Could be. This cliff is too steep for us to climb down though, even if we were mountain goats. And there isn't much of a beach before you get to the waves crashing into the outcrops." She stepped next to Dahlia to look down. Rocks protruded from the water like ancient seats. "Although, those rocks are perfect. Can you imagine mermaids sitting on each of those and combing their hair?"

"And then they swim into their secret caves under the island."

"But not before snatching children away." Rosie grabbed Dahlia and stepped back from the edge, tickling the girl's ribs.

Dahlia laughed, a sound of uncomplicated joy that made Rosie's heart clench. God, she would do anything for this child. They didn't warn you of that—not in all the books she'd read about decorating the nursery or training your child to sleep through the night or figuring out tummy time. No expert thought to point out that Rosie's happiness would forever after be tied up with her child's happiness. That she would do anything to protect her child.

They settled down in the mixture of grass and soft moss to look out over the water and listen to the soothing sound of the surf. Soon Rosie's breath matched the sounds of the ocean. There really was something magic about this place. The elements presented with greater force, giving an impression of wildness. The expanse of the blue sky combined with the rush of wind. No wonder so many Irish fairy tales boasted of supernatural fae or creatures who were able to call on the full force of water, fire, air, and earth.

"Some people lived here." Dally caressed a tiny bundle of yellow flowers with her index finger but didn't pick it.

"Sure." Rosie smiled. Her daughter's insights never ceased to delight. "And they probably liked listening to the water just like us."

"Can we go look at the house?" Dahlia pointed.

Gasping, Rosie reached for her phone to take a picture. "Woah! You don't see things like that back in Baltimore."

The cottage ruins, now that Dally had pointed them out, were impossible to miss. The roof—probably made of overlapping layers of sod with straw thatch from wheat or flax—had disappeared long ago.

Gray rocks, durable as time, stood in a skeleton of a two, no, Rosie corrected herself as she analyzed the structure, three-room cottage. She ducked through the standing doorway and twirled around, Dally coming after.

"We could have lived here, Dally-girl. Grown up with these wildflowers outside your door and the big sky overhead and the lullaby of the ocean. And maybe you would have been a selkie and pulled on your seal skin to swim in the moonlight, free as anybody can be."

Something caught her eye on the wall. Rosie squinted at lines. Ogham? The Celtic "tree language" was used between the fourth and tenth century C.E. She knew of the language—possibly named after the Irish god Oghma—but didn't know enough to recognize any letters. To the side of the lines was a carving. It looked like some kind of animal with a long body and four legs. A cross was marked on its back and it seemed to be wearing a crown. Rosie ran her index finger from the crown's base up to the first pearl, down and then up to the second pearl, down and up to the last pearl.

This was exactly what she'd been hoping to find. Excited, Rosie took more pictures, zooming in so she could examine the details later.

"And then Daddy wouldn't find us?"

Forgetting about the etching, Rosie shoved her phone in her pocket and faced her daughter.

Dahlia stood in the middle of the ruined house and rubbed the hem of her shirt between her thumb and index finger. "His house is by the Atlantic Ocean and this house is by the Atlantic Ocean."

Words stuck in Rosie's throat. She leaned her forehead against the gray rocks that had framed the door, seeking a sense of coolness against her overheated skin. Had there been a happy family in this house? It didn't matter. There was no use comparing one family to another. She had to do the best she could to explain that their situation was not Dahlia's fault.

"The ocean is very large." Rosie straightened and cleared her throat. "You know you and I will always be together, right? But Daddy isn't part of our lives right now because he has to learn not to be so angry."

"Because he breaks things. Even when I'm being very good and quiet."

Rosie closed her eyes remembering one of the last times that Dalia had sat in her room in the shared house playing with her animal figurines. Rosie had pulled her own pink doll castle out of storage and given it to Dally when she turned three. Dally loved the blue drawbridge that had a tiny crank with an actual string attached so it would raise and lower. She made each of the round rooms a stable for an animal family and would tuck them in over and over. Something had happened at Kenny's work—something so trivial Rosie had long ago forgotten—and he'd come home fuming. He'd screamed at Rosie and Dally to clean up the toys, but they hadn't reacted quickly enough, and he'd picked up the entire castle, with figurines inside, and thrown it against the wall. Dally had stood in the bedroom, shaking while pee ran down her leg to puddle on the floor. He apologized later and said he'd find a replacement online. But Rosie would never forget the terrified expression on Dahlia's face as she stared at her father.

"I know." Rosie nodded. "And sometimes he wasn't very thoughtful and made us feel bad inside." *Damn it, Kenny*, Rosie thought. *You've hurt me so many times, but you don't get to hurt Dally.* "Maybe tonight we could write a letter to Daddy? Explain your feelings. I can help you write it, but we won't send it. Would that be, okay?"

Dally's fingers pinched the material her shirt over and over. Finally, she looked up and nodded.

Rosie held out her hand. "Let's go back to town. We're supposed to have dinner at the pub and I'm getting very hungry."

They ducked through the doorway and walked down the pathway past the cottages and then to Main Street. As they came near the bookstore, Dahlia pulled away and ran toward the field behind.

"Look, Mom!"

Rosie followed and came to the flower field that she'd seen from the bathroom window. A run-in shed stood next to the building, so she hadn't been able to see it before. A grey mule nosed through hay, but stopped and came over to Dally. She pet his nose while Rosie looked for a fence—there wasn't one. This mule was simply staying here.

"Pet him!" Dally rubbed the mule's shoulder vigorously.

Rosie moved closer. "This is a strange animal and could be dangerous. You need to check with someone before you rush forward."

"But he's nice." Dally pouted.

"It's not about an animal being nice or mean. It's about their motivation. Does he think you have food? Does he think you are food? Is he scared of you? Are you standing between him and something that he wants?"

"But I could tell that he was happy because of the way his ears moved and then he held out his nose to sniff me."

The mule dropped his head and half-closed his eyes, an expression of bliss that was difficult to deny.

"You're very good with animals, Dally, but you still have to be careful." Rosie rubbed the mule's nose. "He is awfully cute though."

Suddenly, the mule's ears went straight up and he jerked his head to stare into the distance.

Both Rosie and Dahlia whipped their heads around to stare in the same direction. The tall grass undulated as something moved along the ground away from them, heading toward the creek.

"Hee-Hawwww!" The mule let loose an ear-splitting bray of fear and then jerked away, running toward Main Street with his bell clanging.

Rosie gave a surprised laugh and looked at Dahlia to share a smile, but the girl was already tearing through the wildflowers after the mystery creature.

"Come on, Mom," she called. "I want to see whatever it was."

Rosie raced after her. The flowers and grass reached above her knees and it was about forty yards to the creek.

There was a splash of creek water and Dally reached the spot a few seconds later.

Rosie was breathing hard by the time she caught up to her daughter on the muddy edge of the creek. The embankment was about a foot above the clear water. Trees grew tall, reaching their spring time green leaves toward the sky.

"It's gone." Dally sounded disappointed. "It had black eyes like marbles and it looked at me, but then it ran away. I think it went deeper into the forest over there."

The trees on the other side of the creek grew dense and the leaves shut out the sun so it was harder to see. No stores or roads or buildings. Probably not very much land before the island dropped off into the ocean.

"Was it a pig?" Rosie asked, looking around. "A coyote?" The mule had acted terrified. It wouldn't have been a deer. Even a doe would have been taller than the wild flowers.

"No." Dally crossed her arms. "I didn't recognize it from any of my books."

Rosie noticed two tracks in the mud of the embankment in front of the water. "Aha!" She felt quite the detective. "Look there. It must have been a wild dog. That is clearly a dog print with nails."

"It wasn't a dog." Dally radiated skepticism. "It had a long body and was low in the grass and then it ran away and leapt into the water."

Looking closer, the print was almost blurry, as if something connected each of the toes and ruined the straight lines. Unsure, Rosie changed the subject. "All animals are different. The mule was scared of this animal and this guy was scared of us. That's why I told you to be careful."

Dahlia's stomach growled and gurgled. Her eyes widened as she clamped a hand to her belly. Lowering her voice, Dally said, "I'm hungry, Mom. Don't stand between me and food!"

Chapter Four

Rosie didn't know if they needed to change clothes before supper at Sea Monster's Sauce, but they went ahead and washed up before heading over. Dahlia chose a blue sundress and white crocheted sweater. Rosie brushed her daughter's hair and then handed her a headband. The humidity on the island didn't seem to affect Dahlia's hair. It didn't, a rogue part of her mind noted, seem to affect Jordan's black hair either. But her own shoulder-length hair had just enough wave to be a victim. There was nothing she could do without a ton of spray so she left it down. It was their first weekend in Ireland—time to pull out the cute clothing. Rosie slid into a pair of summer pants and a white boatneck shirt. A quick application of mascara and coral lipstick and she was ready.

It was really throwing off her sense of time that it stayed light so late. The summer twilight created a peach haze and the shops along Main Street each boasted baskets of colorful flowers. The towering trees in the forest behind the bookstore produced a stunning dark green backdrop. There was even, Rosie was willing to swear, the faint sound of lapping water coming from the ferry dock a block away.

Most of the tables at the pub were already filled. It was Saturday night and the crowd was boisterous. Rosie held onto Dahlia's hand and glanced around. Windows were open to welcome the night breeze. Animated conversations were everywhere, the Irish accents rising and rolling. Dylan, behind the bar, waved her toward a booth on the side. The other grad students were already there. Erika and Peyton sat on each side of Dimitri, who looked quite pleased with the arrangement.

Rosie let Dally slide in on their side first. "How was your day?"

"Jet lag," said Peyton. "I have no idea what time it is or if I'm supposed to be eating breakfast or dinner."

"Supper," corrected Dylan, appearing at their table. He wore a pair of worn jeans and a t-shirt that stretched tight across his chest. Both Erika and Peyton perked up. "Welcome to the Sauce, the most popular pub on the island."

Dimitri laughed. "The only one on the island, right?"

"There's a bar in the hotel, but here you'll get live music. The island only has about 400 year-round residents so it would be too much effort to compete." Dylan winked at Peyton. "That's why I'm happy to be the liaison with your university."

"You must be glad when girls come over from the mainland… or America," Peyton said, tossing her hair in case she'd been too subtle.

"Where's the dance club?" Dimitri asked.

"On the mainland, obviously, and farther east." Erika rolled her eyes and pulled away from Dimitri. "Didn't you research this place at all when you registered for the program?"

Dylan flashed Erika a smile. His teeth were so white it gave Rosie a flash of jealousy. Didn't he drink coffee?

"You lot are the island's first experiment with the travel abroad program. Hopefully, you'll have a productive experience and we'll be able to expand the program. Suppers and one drink are included. After that, you're on the hook for the drinks. If you're unsure what to order, I'd advise Shepherd's Pie. Mrs. Troutskill's made them and," Dylan kissed his fingers, "they are divine."

"Who is Mrs. Troutskill?" Dimitri asked.

Dally giggled and leaned against Rosie.

"She's a local," Dylan said. "What else can I do to make your stay on the island more productive? I know the young women are coming here after lunch tomorrow so we can talk about understanding your audience and how to create ambiance."

Both Peyton and Erika nodded.

"What about you?" Dylan asked Dimitri. "Business, right? Who can I connect you with?"

"There aren't really any big businesses on this island. It's all mom-and-pop, you know? I'm not sure there's very much for me to learn." Dimitri had his arms spread out, grazing the shoulders of each young woman beside him.

Dylan's smiled dipped a bit, but Rosie silently applauded the way he brought it right back.

"Well, we certainly have many locals with entrepreneurial spirits, but some of us are looking for B2B connections—that's why I partnered with the university to host your lovely group. Tourists come over on the ferry for a day and that's nice, but it's better to have visitors for longer. That way businesses can make better forecasts for purchasing supplies. Makes sense, right?"

He waited for them to nod before adding, "You lot are more reasonable than some people on this island."

Rosie narrowed her eyes. "Who?"

He lifted his eyebrows. "You should know."

Yes, he was definitely alluding to Jordan. Why would she be opposed to having long-term visitors on the island? She needed customers for her bookshop and bakery and flower business. Maybe if there were more customers then she wouldn't have to have a laundry list of things she was willing to sell. That might, Rosie acknowledged with a wince, be a little snarky.

"However, if the construction on the mainland moves forward with the resort, then we'll be able, hopefully, to lure a steady flow of tourists to the island not only during summer but throughout most of the year. It would make a huge difference for the businesses here." He gestured at Dimitri. "We would be able to sponsor another pub. Another hotel." Dylan flashed his white teeth again. "Maybe even a dance club."

"We passed the construction. It's right at the ferry stop." Peyton tilted her head. "What do you mean 'if'?"

"There's been some complaint that the construction is bad for the environment because the project is so close to the shore that it creates more pollution and requires more engineering. The complaints are ridiculous and the crews will get back to work as soon as the inspector signs off." Dylan looked over his shoulder at the bar where several patrons had lined up. "I'll put in your dinner orders and then come back over when there's a lull. Rosie, I didn't forget you." He pointed to her as he backed up toward the bar. "Dally, do you want to feed some farm animals one day so your mom can work?"

"Oh, yes!" Dally said, clasping her hands together and then looking at Rosie for permission.

"Wonderful! Let me pull some draughts and I will be back with your food."

When he was gone, Erika shook her head. "I love the way he speaks. It's like music."

"I love how he's so outgoing. And smart about business trends." Peyton watched him talking to another customer on the way back to the bar. "And how he looks. Not to be shallow."

Dimitri said, "That's the definition of shallow."

"No. It's second-wave feminism. I'm asserting my desires instead of sublimating them."

"That sounds very smart," Dimitri said, "but maybe work on devaluing appearance and concentrating on substance."

Having no desire to debate, Rosie didn't mention that Dylan's accent seemed emphasized when he'd been talking to their table. Instead, she took the opportunity to people watch. Most customers seemed to be in work clothing. Islanders, then. But some conversations had a range of tones and sounds. Those would be visitors. Rosie could hear the differences but wasn't able to identify which geographic area the accents were from. Overall, glasses were half-full, people leaned over the low tables, the smell of good, hearty food permeated the air. Now her stomach was growling.

Mrs. Troutskill pushed through the swinging door carrying a tray.

Dally gaped. "You work here, too?"

"No, dearie. Just filling in for my niece. She's got a bit of a cold." She set the tray down. "Who was smart enough to order my Shepherd's Pie?"

Everyone except Dimitri raised their hand.

Each plate held an enormous serving of meat and cooked vegetables between thick layers of mashed potatoes. The top had ridges from where Mrs. Troutskill had smoothed the potatoes and the crust was a deep golden brown.

"This is Instagram-worthy," Peyton said, pulling out her phone.

"Thank you... I think." Mrs. Troutskill delivered the last plate to Dimitri with a steak, mashed potatoes, and asparagus. "Here's for you, young man. Dylan has been ordering more meat that usual. That's fresh butchered from my herd."

"Uh. That's a little too much information." Dimitri's face paled. "I like to think of my food as coming from a grocery store."

"How do you think I get supplies for my grocery store, young man?" Mrs. Troutskill pulled down her glasses to examine him. Satisfied when he wouldn't meet her gaze, Mrs. Troutskill turned to Dally. "I understand you're coming to my farm. I have ducks and chickens. The birds are terribly spoiled, and you'll need to clean both the little pool and the coop. The ewes just had lambs, though, and you won't mind petting them. I also have two fainting goats. Friendly as anything. I don't need 'em, but they make me laugh and that's worth their keep. My sister has an old mare in one pasture and the cows in the other. There's a lot of work."

"I've always wanted to live on a farm." Dahlia wiggled in her seat. "We don't have any pets at home."

"Always?" Mrs. Troutskill tapped Dahlia's head. "How old are you, dearie?"

"Six."

"Well, I suppose six years is a long time to be wantin' something. You're welcome on my farm, but I'm off for now." Mrs. Troutskill sighed as she untied the strings of her apron. "Too bad you don't have a twin."

With the line at the bar under control, Dylan walked over to the microphone in the corner and pulled a stool up to it.

"Good evening, folks." He waited to be acknowledged by at least of few of the patrons. "It's Saturday night on the island. We have some tourists here and we have some visitors from America. Let's toast."

Rosie and the other students found themselves reaching for glasses as most of the people in the pub turned to look at them and called out, "Slainte!"

After they all took a drink, Dylan sank onto the stool and adjusted his microphone. "Now, Rosie, this is for you. A tale to begin the night."

Dally grinned at her and Rosie couldn't help feeling special.

"We're different than America where the buildings are considered old and get their little historic plaques if they are from the Revolutionary War. But here we live with our past. So when we see ruins, we remember." He took a drink of Guinness and continued. "The hills are entrances to the Otherworld and we can still see traces of the Tuatha De Danann. Well, what you might not know is they were a supernatural race who look like humans but never age and never get sick. They also have powers of magic." He lowered his voice. "There is a prophecy they will return—they will come back ready for battle to help Ireland in her time of greatest need."

Rosie dug for a pen in her purse. Why hadn't she been ready? This was the perfect opportunity to record a new story from a local. She could compare the oral storytelling to what was written in textbooks. Would this be about the four gifts? Maybe a more specific story about the Sword of Nuada, the Spear of Lugh, the Cauldron of the Dagda, or the Lia Fail?

"You could get closer and use your phone to record him," Erika whispered.

Relief rushed through her. "That's brilliant. Thank you!" Rosie made her way through the crowded pub.

A rush of cold air swept past her as the pub door opened. A group of three people walked in carrying instruments. And there, shutting the door, was Jordan. Her dark hair was swept back in some type of bun while bangs were gelled at an angle across her forehead. Even in the pub's dim lighting Rosie could see her grey eyes.

"Hop over, Dylan," Jordan called.

"I'm right in the middle of a story," he protested.

Jordan held up the violin case in her hand and asked the pub. "Do you want him to finish or do you want us to play?"

Immediately customers roared for music, some with teasing comments to Dylan to get back behind the counter and serve drinks.

Dylan stood up, but leaned close to the microphone to say, "Sorry, Rosie. The crowd has spoken and I must obey." He held his hands up in a classic shrugging motion.

The musicians moved to set up, but Jordan took a moment to look toward the table of Americans. Her gaze landed, briefly, on Rosie before Jordan brought her attention back to her violin and laughed at something the man holding a tin whistle said.

Rosie stood still in the center of the pub, holding her phone and wondering what the hell just happened. The conversations around her blurred so it was hard to pick out individual voices. Then a waitress pushed past her carrying a tray loaded with empty glasses and bottles. Rosie shook her head. She needed to get out of the way. And this opportunity could still be recovered.

She pushed her way up to the bar.

"Hey, there," Dylan greeted her. "Ready for a drink? Remember the second one you have to pay for."

She waved her hand. "I want to hear the rest of your story."

"Sure." He set glasses under taps and began the process of building a Guinness. "Maybe one afternoon when the pub is quiet."

"Thank you." She nodded. "I'll take a glass of red wine now. After all, I don't have to drive home."

Careful not to spill, Rosie made her way back to the booth and slid in next to Dally.

"How are you doing? Bored?"

"No, not yet," Dahlia said. She patted her stomach. "That dinner was so good. Why don't you ever make something like that?"

Rosie smiled. "It was good."

Just then a crash of thunder shook the building and lightning flashed through the windows. A second later, rain began falling in a deluge. People near windows moved to pull them closed and then the music began as if to drive away the weather.

Rosie had been to music concerts before, but nothing like this. The mix of pipes, fiddle, and four-stringed banjo blasted through the pub. Jordan took the lead, stepping out in front. The rhythm was fast and reckless; her fingers blurred as they moved over the neck of her fiddle. The intensity swelled so that Rosie sat up straighter in her seat. Just as she couldn't take another second of the fiddle's music, Jordan stopped playing and sang instead.

Her voice was haunting. Though the words were in Gaelic, Rosie felt like she could almost understand, but not quite. It was a ballad, there was clearly a story unfolding, and the pub fell quiet as everyone hung, suspended in whatever spell Jordan cast. Then she took a step back from the microphone and applause erupted.

At their table, Dimitri leaned forward to the group. "Her voice is spectacular, but why is she wearing such a long skirt? Why not something more sexy?"

No one bothered answering, but it reminded Rosie that while Jordan sometimes wore sleeveless tailored shirts, she did always wear trousers or calf-length skirts. She mentally shrugged. Probably just her style.

Jordan began fiddling again, but it must have been a crowd favorite because this time the pub sang the chorus with her. Rosie sipped on her wine and let herself be swept up in the swell of the music. It was magic, but part of her was still an observer. She watched the musicians play and Dylan pouring, and the customers telling stories, but she was also alone, invisible.

Erika touched her shoulder and leaned closer. "I said, we're heading out. The musicians are on break and the storm is over."

"Of course." Rosie and Dally slid off the bench. "It's time for us to go too."

She followed the other Americans to the front door, Dally in front of her. This meant that they walked right in front of Jordan and the band. Rosie kept her gaze forward.

"Anne-Rose?"

Rosie, hand still on Dally, looked over at Jordan, trying to think of something to say about how wonderful the music had been or how she hadn't known Jordan was so talented.

Jordan, effortlessly cool, held the neck of a green bottle in one hand. They were standing inches apart, but Rosie couldn't read her expression.

"I saw you and Dahlia in back with Manny today."

Manny? Ah, she must mean the mule. "Yes, we were—"

"Don't go back there."

All thoughts of complimenting Jordan disappeared. "We were careful of the flowers, if that's what you're worried about." Well, except when they'd run toward the creek chasing the dog. But why was it any of Jordan's business? She didn't own the whole island, although she probably did own the land behind the bookstore.

"There's ticks," Jordan said. "And other things. It's not for tourists. Stick to the cliffs and the town."

"Or what?" Rosie knew it was a childish taunt, but Jordan made her so angry.

"Or you won't like what you find." Jordan raised the green bottle. "Slainte."

Chapter Five

Dahlia's scream ripped through the night.

Rosie jumped from the bed, but her legs tangled in the sheets and she landed painfully on her knees.

"I'm here," she called to Dally through the darkness. "It's okay." She crawled along the floor to the table and pulled herself up, switching the lamp on.

Gentle light illuminated the bedroom. Dally sat up straight in bed with eyes wide open but unfocused. With closed fists she hit herself in the face and chest.

Rosie rushed over and sat on the bed next to her daughter, cupping the girl's hands in her own.

"You're okay," she soothed, the way the doctor had told her to. "Mommy's here."

It had been months since the last night terror. The episodes had been frequent after they'd run from Kenny. Then there was the period when they'd had to change everything—moving to a new place, getting a new job—so he wouldn't find them. Finally, they'd been able to settle into a routine. The night terrors had become less frequent and had finally gone away. Until tonight.

Tears ran down Dally's face and her body rocked back and forth. That was okay—the doctor said it was a way to self-sooth.

Rosie kept up her affirmations in a calm voice. Gradually, Dally's fists released, and she slumped over, eyes closed.

Exhaling, Rosie let her own head drop.

"Mommy?"

"Hi, sweetie." Relief swept through Rosie at the natural tone of Dally's voice. "You had a bad dream, but you're okay now."

Dahlia turned to her side, looking fragile and young with her brown hair spread across the pillow. "I don't want him to come into our territory."

Rosie's blood turned to splinters of ice inside as fear became a physical pain. She hadn't left Dahlia alone at all. It was always the two of them. Did she mean Kenny? What other 'he'? And what did she mean 'territory'?

Dahlia turned again so she was on her back and her eyes met Rosie's. "If he comes again, I'm going to bite him."

What was she talking about? Was this from a movie or something her class had talked about?

"Shh, sweetie," Rosie said, smoothing Dally's hair back. "It's time to sleep now."

Dahlia obediently closed her eyes. Rosie sat beside her on the bed until the girl's breath evened out.

Easing off the bed, Rosie headed to the bathroom. That's what she got for having a glass of wine at the pub. Her mouth was dry and she needed to pee.

Hand on the bathroom light switch, Rosie paused. There—out the window—a flicker of white in the field. Rosie moved closer to the window and peered out. A figure in a dark coat, holding a lantern, was crossing the field toward the creek. The light moved back and forth as if the figure searched for something. The tall trees of the forest moved in the wind, a residue from the storm earlier. The figure lifted the lantern higher as they picked their way across the rocks in the creek. As they did, the cloud cover blew away and the light of the moon clearly shone on the figure's face: Jordan.

Rosie ducked away from the window so she wouldn't be seen, heart beating fast. After a few seconds, she peeked out again. There was a brief flicker of light from the woods and then it disappeared. Rosie used the bathroom and went back to bed, her mind bouncing between Dahlia's cryptic remarks after the night terror and figuring out why the fiddle-playing, bookstore-managing, myth-interrupting woman was wandering around the island in the middle of the night in the very place that she'd told them not to go.

∞

The next morning Rosie and Dahlia went downstairs to the café together. Yes, it was Sunday morning. Yes, they should go to church. It would be another opportunity to meet island residents and experience more traditions. But even though Dahlia hadn't had another night terror, Rosie hadn't been able to fall back asleep. She needed coffee, maybe some oatmeal, and some time to make a daily plan because she had to start working FOR REAL on Monday.

"Good morning, girls," Mrs. Troutskill called from her seat at the counter in front of the expresso machine. A yellow-and-white cake sat to the side. "You're just in time."

Jordan, not looking like she'd been up all night traipsing about, appeared effortlessly chic in a russet blouse with a y-neckline that showed off the thick chain necklace that matched her earrings.

"Coffee?" Jordan asked. Rosie stared at her, wondering if she'd imagined last night. Well, she certainly hadn't imagined the part where Jordan had shut down the myth-telling.

"Yes, please. A cappuccino."

"Hot chocolate for me, please," Dahlia said, climbing onto a stool next to Mrs. Troutskill and resting her chin in her hands. "It was a rough night."

"Oh?" Mrs. Troutskill adjusted her glasses. "I'm sorry to hear that. Perhaps Jordan can be enjoined to make you blueberry pancakes as well as the drink."

"I don't cook." Jordan poured the milk into the steamer. "That's your sister's job."

"There's a cake right there." Dahlia's eyebrows pulled together. "Aren't you Mrs. Bakery?"

Mrs. Troutskill laughed, delighted. "My sister made the milk cake, but I get to share it with the kitties. That's what I meant when I said you arrived at the right time."

"Oh," Dahlia perked up. "May I take it in to them? That will make me feel tons better."

The grinding of espresso beans was followed by the whir of the machine. The distinctive smell of ground coffee and warm milk filled the café. Rosie closed her eyes to appreciate the aroma. Her stomach rumbled. Embarrassed, Rosie moved toward the oatmeal and used the ladle to serve herself.

"Do you feel happier because you're helping Mrs. Troutskill or because the animals feel happy?" Jordan asked Dally.

Rosie frowned as she sprinkled brown sugar over the oats. That was a very nuanced question for a child who had just finished first grade.

"Both," Dally said, her childish voice sincere. She'd picked up the cake and was carrying it, wobbling, across the floor. "But mostly because I like when animals are happy."

She continued her deliberate steps toward the cat café, right foot forward and left up to join.

"How do you know whether an animal is happy or not? Maybe you just think they are."

"That's silly," Dally said. She turned to give Jordan a look over her shoulder. "They purr or snort or snuffle or they eyeroll or their ears go back."

Mrs. Troutskill burst into laughter.

Jordan leaned out from behind the expresso machine to give the other islander a withering look.

"Good girl," Mrs. Troutskill said to Dahlia. "Now, do you want me to open the door so you can feed the kitties in their play area?"

"No," Dally said, lowering the cake to the floor near the cat entrance under the counter looking out across Main Street. "They can come out if they want. I'll wait to play until they've finished eating."

Mrs. Troutskill slapped the back counter with her palm. "Oh, that's rich. Jordan, you've met someone more sensitive than yourself. And she's an American. That must stick in your craw."

"I assure you," Jordan set two mugs in front of Rosie, "there's nothing stuck in my craw."

"Dahlia, it's time for you to come eat, too," Rosie called. "Maybe a piece of fruit?"

Irish Teddy poked his handsome head out of the cat door and spied the cake. Then he ducked back inside the play area.

"He must not like your sister's cake," Jordan said.

"He's getting the others," Dally said confidently.

They all watched as Irish Teddy went around to the various nooks and crannies of the play area with his message. Then, like the Pied Piper, he led the cats through the cat door to settle around the cake pan.

Dahlia's eyes shone as she watched them eat, their pink tongues flicking, their whiskers twitching, her attention locked on the pattern of movement as the cats jockeyed for position.

"Do the cats most often stay out here in the café or in their play area?" Rosie asked as she stirred the oatmeal, waiting for it to cool.

Jordan shrugged one shoulder. "They are free to go wherever they want."

"And that doesn't cause any problems with your customers?" She took a bite. The oatmeal tasted as good as it smelled. "No one has allergies or steps on a cat's tail?"

"If there is any problem in my clearly titled Cat Café then I side with my animals." Jordan had both hands on the counter and leaned forward for emphasis, her grey eyes meeting Rosie's. "I always side with animals. The humans can leave."

"Yeah, you'd like that wouldn't you!" Rosie stood up so fast that the spoon from her oatmeal clattered to the floor. "I don't know why you agreed to be a host if you don't want visitors to the island."

Mrs. Troutskill looked back and forth between them. "Dahlia, let's go feed Manny the mule. He's staying behind the grocery for a couple days and I bet he's hungry."

Eyes wide, Dally looked to Rosie for approval.

Unnerved by her own outburst, Rosie nodded. "Come right back afterward."

"I will."

Jordan and Rosie stared at each other in silence until the tinkling bell signaled that they were alone.

Frustratingly calm, Jordan handed Rosie a new spoon. "There are plenty of places in Ireland where you can visit castles and listen to music and go to clubs or explore museums. If you're interested in myths, you should be planning a trip to see The Book of Kells. This country has so many beautiful libraries, you can get lost in them for days. But here," Jordan shook her head, "this is a small island full of people and animals who've lived here for generations. We keep to the old ways. There are reasons for it and I don't need to explain them to strangers."

Rosie paced in the café and when she got to the side door, she stopped to look at the corkboard there with the Wi-Fi password posted and the rest open for local advertisements or photos from visitors. There, in the corner, was a postcard featuring Baltimore's Inner Harbor. Ironic. You could visit halfway around the world and someone had already been there before you.

Pivoting, Rosie stalked back toward Jordan. "Everyone on this island has secrets!"

"So do you, Anne-Rose." Jordan gestured at her. "You're here for weeks to get an intensive paper written—a paper you claim determines whether you get a new job. Why then would you bring a child with you? I see you worrying about her breakfast and figuring out what she can do so that you can work without feeling guilty. Why isn't she with her father? Her grandparents? What's your secret?"

It would feel so good to tell a stranger—someone that she'd never see again after this trip —and maybe it would wipe that smug look off Jordan's face.

"We ran away from my ex-husband because he was abusive but no one believed me. My parents were so happy because his family had banking ties to Switzerland—that's where his family is from—and he took me to the family house in Grindelwald and proposed on the ski slopes. His father videoed it and we sent it to my parents. It was incredibly romantic, like I was in a movie or something. So, later, when I told them about our fights, they thought I must be exaggerating or doing something wrong. They kept saying how perfect the proposal had been."

Jordan picked up the empty coffee cup and rinsed it out. Then she steamed more milk.

The lump in Rosie's throat hurt, but she kept going. "And his parents... they'd seemed really nice. They took us out to dinners at their country club and brought flowers when they visited me in the hospital the first time..."

"First time?" Jordan interrupted.

Rosie couldn't stop now, not when the words were spilling out: "We—Kenny and I—said I'd fallen. But after Dally was born, I wanted to be a happy family. I wanted to go to a therapist or something. So the next time, I showed his mom the bruises." She rubbed her forearm as she remembered his hand wrapped around it and his face strangely blank as he'd shaken her. What had she done that time to set him off? The house had to be clean, the baby had to be bathed, dinner had to be hot, she had to be ready if he wanted to go to bed.

"Drink." Jordan set the refilled cappuccino in front of her. "It's a little early, but say the word and I'll pour a shot of whiskey in."

"This is good." Rosie brought the mug to her mouth and drank, finding the warm liquid comforting. "Kenny said it was his job as the head of our house to punish me if I ever didn't do what he wanted. His mom knew. I saw it on her face. She even hugged me. I thought this was the breakthrough we all needed."

"So she told him that you and the baby would live in their house while he saw a therapist or got on medication or listened to whatever the professionals suggested?"

"I was so stupid." Rosie scoffed. "His mom invited me over for a meeting with her husband and she was like a different person. She said that I'd forced them to choose between their son and me. Of course, they would choose their son. Then Kenny Sr. said if I ever tried to ruin their son's reputation then they'd make my life hell." Rosie set the mug on the counter. "They had papers to sign. They said if I agreed then I could have full custody of Dahlia and they'd give me money to start over."

Jordan nodded. "So you took their money and now you get to chase fairy tales in Ireland."

"No!" Rosie glared at Jordan. "I told them to keep their filthy money and went to the police station to file a restraining order."

"I see." Jordan's grey eyes studied Rosie.

"Do you?" Rosie could hear that she was yelling, but she'd lost control. "Because I don't think that you understand what's it like to start over with a new name and a new job and a little girl who keeps crying because she wants her old name. Meanwhile, you're so scared that your husband is going to find you and beat the crap out of you for making him look bad that you look at every car that follows you for too long and you switch grocery stores so you don't become predictable. And you can't call your parents for advice about your daughter's teething because they'll tell where you are. And you definitely can't let your in-laws babysit for a weekend because they'll take your child away." Rosie's chest heaved. "No one would ever believe you."

"So you have no family. No community. No one you can trust."

Rosie hung her head. "I did it for Dahlia. Because I knew what made him mad and I could have avoided those things or talked him down, maybe. But Dahlia is my baby. And I wasn't going to ever let her be scared of being hit or watch her running to hide or even living to make someone else happy. So I made that sacrifice to give up security and comfort and everything I knew. And I would do it again." Rosie lifted her head, pressing on because she was tired of hiding the truth. "Because if my ex raised a hand against her... I would kill him."

"I believe you." Jordan said it like a pledge.

Rosie gave a bitter laugh. "That I would kill someone?"

"Everything." Jordan continued in the same serious tone. "I believe that you were abused. I believe you tried to make it work. I believe, sadly, that your family members who should have protected you chose not to."

The words—words she'd longed to hear for so long—undid the knot inside of Rosie's throat. Tears spilled down her cheeks and her shoulders shook with sobs.

Jordan walked over to the napkins and returned, offering one. "You can't, you know."

"Thanks." Rosie took one more bracing breath and then wiped her cheeks. "What do you mean?"

"You think that you can prevent your husband's temper by getting rid of all the triggers so that he doesn't experience any pain or frustration. You think that if you do this, then he'll be a decent man. But you're wrong. The world doesn't care about your ex, and you can't absorb all the pain that will come to him. The only thing he can do is become resilient. And that's his learning curve, not yours. The more you try to protect him, the more he'll lose any ability to recover from frustrations, disappointments, and failures. So stop trying to be a martyr. I think you're very brave to have walked away and started over."

Laughter bubbled up out of Rosie. It was like the crying had broken something open inside. She was a mess.

"What's so funny?" Jordan tilted her head.

Rosie shook her head. Maybe she shouldn't say anything, but she had no energy left to filter. "I was so pissed off at you because I was trying to record Dylan's myth in the pub last night. That was my first bit of local research—I was hoping for a story from this island that had never been recorded before—and you walked in and pushed him away from the microphone. Now you're being incredibly nice and the juxtaposition is giving me whiplash!"

"Ahhh, that's why you were blowing an attitude when you left the pub." Jordan walked out from behind the café counter. "Follow me."

Jordan led the way to the other part of the store. As soon as they stepped into the room Rosie had to stop herself from gaping. Walnut-stained shelves lined the room with stacks in the middle. A ladder on the widest wall allowed access to the higher books while plants hung from the ceiling, tendrils interlacing as if the plants were holding hands. On the back wall a bay window with pillow seating looked out over the meadow. Two tables offered workspace by the soft glow of elegant lamps.

"This room is exquisite," Rosie said, twirling around to take in all the details.

Jordan scanned the bookshelf between windows that looked out on the main street. "Ah ha," she said, victorious. She handed a thick book to Rosie titled *A Treasury of Irish Myth, Legend, and Folklore*. "William Butler Yeats collected the folktales and Lady Gregory arranged the second part of the Cuchulain story."

"Right," Rosie licked her lips. Jordan was being so friendly that Rosie didn't want to hurt her feelings by pointing out that she didn't need to read any more folktales, she wanted to collect new ones for comparison. She slid the book onto the worktable. "I have research already."

Jordan looked from the book back at Rosie. "Well, if you want to hear the end of Dylan's tale, you can read it there. My guess is he was telling the part from Cuchulain's courting of Emer." She smiled. "But you bend the pages then you've bought the book. I'm running a store here, not a library."

Realization hit Rosie. "Wait. Dylan wasn't telling a tale specific to this island? He reads collections and then acts like he knows the myths? His mom didn't tell him the stories when he a little boy?" Her cheeks flushed red as her impression of Dylan shifted. "He's a fake. A liar. A charlatan."

"Aww, don't be mad at Dylan. That's what he does." Jordan gave her a sympathetic look. "He's not even from the island. Honestly, I think his mum lives outside of Liverpool."

Rosie sank into the nearby chair. She whispered, "But I thought he was the real thing."

"Do you want the real thing?" Jordan gave her a lopsided smile. "Sometimes it's right under your nose."

"What do you mean?"

"Nothing." Jordan waved her hand in dismissal. "So what exactly are you studying?"

Remembering the other graduate students' boredom, Rosie shook her head. "I don't think—"

"I'll do my own thinking," Jordan said tartly.

"Fine. I'm interested in the gender roles of the characters in Celtic mythology. What does it mean when characters with the same name act differently in versions of the same myth? My idea is that story elements might be reduced to something like the Stith-Thompson Motif Index, but the economic factors, social changes, political ideals, and natural resources of a land also contributed to the relationship between storytellers and their audience."

"You don't look Irish." Jordan crossed her arms across her chest. "Why are you so interested in these stories?"

"My grandparents are Ukrainian. They immigrated to America with my mother to escape antisemitism. There's something about the Irish stories of magic and connection," she tapped her knuckles to her chest, "to the land that resonates with me. When an Irish leader, regardless of gender, did what was right then the land was fertile. When they were selfish or unjust then everyone was punished."

"You're quite the romantic, aren't you?"

"I don't know. It's a different way to see the world. A deeper connection to land, food, traditions than many busy Americans might realize." Rosie sighed. "That's what the colors of the Ukrainian flag mean: yellow represents the ocean of grain shared with the world and the blue represents the sky overhead that stretches over everyone."

Nodding, Jordan moved around the room plucking books off shelves, her long skirt swaying with the graceful movements.

"These two will give you some native insight from Irish authors, one mainlander whose grandmother lived here and one written by an islander. It was never published, but she had it bound in a bookmaker's shop. Might help you make a question list for anyone you want to interview."

"Thank you," Rosie said, rubbing her hands together. She'd been so wrong about both Jordan and Dylan: the one who had seemed unfriendly was going out of her way to help and the one who'd offered to help was a fake. She could usually trust her instincts, but something about all the secrets on this island was throwing her off.

Jordan turned to go and then, uncharacteristically, looked uncertain as she turned back around and studied Rosie's face.

Surprised, Rosie smiled. "What?"

"I thought of one more book that might be useful. It's hard to decipher because it's handwritten in Gaelic. I typed a copy and attached it to the back a long time ago, but it's still in Gaelic. One of the first assignments Saoirse gave me." Jordan's voice caught. "It's an original. You certainly won't find it listed in any of your academic journals."

Excited at the prospect of reading such a special source, Rosie assured her, "I have gloves to prevent oils from hurting the paper."

Jordan's shoulders relaxed and she closed her eyes as if trying to hold back a smile. "That's not what worries me."

"I'll keep it away from the windows and the humidity in here is already controlled…"

"Oh, Anne-Rose, it's the smartest ones who are inclined to pay the doctor instead of the butcher." Jordan walked to the other wall and pulled the ladder into place, climbing up to reach a shelf.

Pay the butcher? For good food instead of a doctor for medicine? "I don't understand that proverb that you just used. Is this about the oatmeal I had for breakfast?"

"Stop talking, Anne-Rose." Jordan pulled a small booklet down. It was slightly bigger than her palm and the edges were tattered. "See what you can make of this. It might be helpful for what you want."

Jordan held it out, but when Rosie took it, the woman wouldn't let go. Almost as if she'd changed her mind.

Finally, Rosie gave an extra tug and Jordan released.

"Have a care," she said. "I'll be in the café."

Grinning, Rosie set the booklet down. Progress! Access to an old handwritten booklet on an isolated island. It would take time to translate the Gaelic, but maybe Jordan would help if she got stuck. She needed her computer, book gloves, post-it notes, and highlighters, but drinking those two cups of coffee meant first a trip to the W.C. Spotting a door that blended into the dark wood underneath the stairs, Rosie twisted the handle.

Oops! Not a W.C., but a coat closet. As she started to shut the door, Rosie noticed something had dripped on the closet floor. Opening the door, she knelt down. A pair of heavy boots were still wet with a bit of flower stuck on one. This must have been what Jordan was wearing on her mysterious walk last night. Reaching inside to touch the boot, Rosie felt a splash on her hand. Red. Thick. The liquid ran across her hand and down to the floor. Holding back a scream, Rosie looked up at the dark cloak.

The hem was soaked in blood.

Chapter Six

As the week passed, Rosie and Dally worked out a routine: after eating breakfast at the café, Dally played with cats while Rosie typed at the counter, and then they walked to the cliff together. After that, Rosie walked Dally to the Troutskill farm so she could help with the afternoon chores and Rosie would work until Mrs. Troutskill—one of them—brought Dally to the pub in time for supper. The afternoon hours had become one of Rosie's favorite parts of the day. Not only were the manuscripts that Jordan had provided an incredible resource of authentic daily life, but something had changed in Jordan's demeanor ever since their fight. While Rosie wouldn't say she was treated like an islander, Jordan was definitely friendlier. That made watching Jordan in action with the tourists who came into the café-bookstore especially entertaining.

There was the man who wouldn't stop asking Jordan out on a date until she pretended to be Dally's mother and asked her "daughter" to please feed Irish Teddy. The man, flustered, left a tip for his coffee and then fled the café while the Rosie, Jordan, and Dally had a laugh. Then there were the tourists who came in and immediately called Jordan "Saoirse" since it was the name of the café. Or the tourists chattering about the "mistake" of the Midsummer sales that the vendors were running when everyone knew that the middle of summer was July. Jordan had explained a few times that Midsummer meant the summer solstice, not the middle of summer, but then just let her eyes go blank and the tourists feel like they'd gotten one over on the Islanders. But there was also a visitor who'd stopped by and caused Jordan to step out from behind the counter and flip the store's sign to 'closed.' From her position in the café, Rosie had seen them going up the stairs to Jordan's private rooms. Nearly thirty minutes later Jordan came down alone and reopened the café. Unable to control her curiosity, Rosie had asked what that was about. Jordan had given that half-smile that wasn't quite a smirk as she said, "Guess that was Saoirse, wasn't it then?"

Unsure whether she was being teased, Rosie had gone back to her pile of books.

Today, though, Rosie was off on an adventure to the mainland.

"You're sure you don't mind?" Rosie asked Mrs. Troutskill again as she shoved her computer into her bag. Where was the cord? Already packed. "I really appreciate it."

"Oh, Dahlia's doing us a favor," Mrs. Troutskill smiled at the girl. "All the animals love her. Especially Manny."

"I love him so much," Dally said. "And he loves me."

Rosie thrust highlighters into her bag. It was true—she'd been amazed to see Dally riding the mule bareback around town the other day. She'd had a helmet on, thank goodness, but it was still surprising to see her little girl in a sundress, bare feet, and a huge grin looking like one of the locals. Why, though, had Manny moved from his little stable behind the café to the Troutskills? She kept meaning to ask.

The door to the café opened and Peyton walked in. She looked run-down with circles under her eyes. It was more than that, though. Her usual confidence was missing.

"Oh, hey, Rosie." Peyton swallowed as she noticed Dahlia and Mrs. Troutskill. "Do you have a minute?"

"I'm about to leave."

Peyton shifted her feet as she looked around the café. "How's your research going? Like, I'm supposed to have an internship with Dylan, but I'm just working for free, you know? I could be serving drinks back home and I'd be making a lot more money."

Mrs. Troutskill shook her head and made a *tsk*ing sound but Rosie couldn't tell if it was judgement toward Dylan or Peyton.

"That's what an internship is," Rosie said. "You're supposed to be getting experience."

"Yeah," Peyton nodded. "But do you like your room?"

"It's great. Dally and I love our room."

"Because ours kinda sucks. Dylan wrote the description that the university used and he exaggerated the amenities. You know?"

"Dahlia and I love our room," Rosie repeated.

The silence stretched.

"You better hurry, Anne-Rose. The ferry won't wait for you," Jordan appeared in the doorway of the café wearing what Rosie had come to recognize as an Aran dress—a tunic crocheted with a diamond stitch by one of the islanders with local wool. The top 'V' and cuffs both had a different, looser stitch that revealed a hint of skin. Despite the heat, Jordan wore a pair of black leggings underneath. Rosie remembered Dimitri's remark about Jordan never showing her legs and then shook it off. It was no one's business and it wasn't like Jordan didn't always look gorgeous. Her large grey eyes, pale skin, and dark hair stood out against the cream color of the tunic. "It's the Summer Solstice so there are extra tourists today."

"I guess I should go too." Peyton looked around the café as if she wanted an excuse to linger and then, finally, left.

After the door shut, Jordan said, "He does have a type, doesn't he?"

"You should probably tell your friend not to mix romance with business, but young people never listen," Mrs. Troutskill said.

Remembering how nasty Peyton had acted about the rented rooms at the beginning, Rosie said, "I'm sure she's fine."

"Anyway, the ferry'll be running twice if not thrice today," Mrs. Troutskill said sagely. "But where are you off to?"

Rosie held up the handwritten booklet and waved it before sliding it back in the special carrying case. "I've been using a combination of a Gaelic dictionary and Google translate, but it's slow going because all the nuance is lost. There's a king with a magic blanket made from the pelt of an animal called a dobhar-chu and the blanket protects anyone who is attacked. The dobhar-chu is a monster nicknamed the 'Irish Crocodile.'"

Mrs. Troutskill looked from the booklet to Jordan. Her voice was sharp as she said, "That looks an awful lot like Old Maude's Diary."

Rosie picked up another of the books that Jordan had lent her and waved it in the air. "This has local eyewitness stories about the creature and both places are nearby. So I'm off to investigate today."

Jordan said to Mrs. Troutskill, "A man's got to do what a man has got to do. Women must do what *they* can't."

Aware that they were having a conversation without her, Rosie let her hand drop. "What's happening?"

"Do you have an umbrella?" Jordan asked her. "It's going to rain later." She shoved a green umbrella at her and Rosie took it instinctively, knowing it was a distraction.

"Here now, give your daughter a kiss." Rosie obediently hugged Dally and looked into her eyes. "Love you."

"Love you too, Mom."

"You won't miss anything during the day. That's all just trinkets and silliness. Us locals will be celebrating at the Midsummer *ceili* tonight." Mrs. Troutskill took Rosie by the shoulders and pushed her toward the café's door. "See you there."

"Wait. What?" Rosie hadn't even realized it was June 21st. That is, she'd realized but hadn't matched the date to the significance of Irish myth and culture. She had so many questions.

The ferry's foghorn sounded a warning.

Uggg. She would have to save them for later. Rosie adjusted her bag and waved her arm in acknowledgement as she rushed outside and into her car.

Once on the ferry, Rosie unlocked the doors, undid her seatbelt, and put the car in park. This time, there was no eerie fog; instead, the sun was shining and the water was a beautiful green-blue. And it was raining. Just a smattering across the windshield. Rosie chuckled. The weather really was complete chaos. Maybe she wasn't an islander, but she wasn't a complete newbie anymore and that felt really good.

The ferry pulled away from the dock.

Okay, time to get organized. Rosie opened her bag, humming as she looked for the notebook. Her thoughts, though, circled back to how easily Ms. Troutskill had invited her to the "real" Midsummer celebrations this evening. And she'd even been able to recognize that Jordan's dress was handmade. And the pattern local. An image of Jordan flashed through her mind. The little half-smile she did when she was acting superior. The sardonic lift to her brow when a tourist came in and said something silly. The way her eyes would flit away if she was bored but could pierce you when interested. Which made Rosie desperate to keep her interested. The way she'd stalked through the bookstore pulling books for Rosie. As each memory floated through, Rosie felt like she'd seen Jordan before.

Abruptly, the image came. Yes, the bookshop manager had been younger with a pixie cut, but those grey eyes, the milk white skin, and haughty expression were the same. Jordan Rooney had been on the cover of *Newsweek Magazine* back when Rosie still lived with Kenny. Jordan had been named the leader of a group of criminals arrested for breaking into a laboratory and freeing the dogs and monkeys that were part of a scientific experiment. The company, of course, had pressed charges, but the pictures of shaved animals with large pleading eyes—some no longer able to walk—had seared Rosie. That image of an unrepentant Jordan had started an international conversation about the abuse of animal testing... and then interest died as something new grabbed headlines.

The mainland came into sight, mountains in the background and green hills in the fore, with a series of shops, hotels, and businesses that looked crowded after staying on the island. Progress had been made on the construction area too, Rosie noted as she pulled her car forward and took the roundabout toward Glenade Lough. It wasn't a long drive and soon enough she pulled into the parking lot near the northern end. Cars filled most of the lot and a family hunched under umbrellas to eat at one of the picnic tables off to the side. Rain splattered on the empty playground of swings and slides and what looked like a small zipline with a seat attached. Dahlia would have enjoyed playing there.

Rosie shrugged into her windbreaker and checked the laces on her hiking boots. First stop: Glencar Waterfall. As soon as she entered the woods, the thick leaves overhead filtered the rain and Rosie pulled back her hood. Mud on the path sucked at her boots, but the air smelled clean. A moment later the rain stopped entirely, and the sun burst out, light catching the droplets so that everything sparkled. Rosie walked out on the viewing platform and gulped. A rainbow crossed the sky overhead; water rushed far below with a dull roar. She knew she was imaginative, but this place, this moment, felt like magic. Everything was shades of green and dark shadow. If she spread her arms then she'd float, suspended between the water and sky. Swaying, Rosie grabbed onto the wooden rail. Today, she was chasing the story of a sea monster that had been sighted at this freshwater lake in 1722, decades before America became a country. This waterfall would have been roaring and the giant trees reaching and the sky unending overhead. It did not seem so strange, suddenly, to imagine an ancient monster had made this its home.

Rosie left the platform and continued down the path. Today was much different than her research back home. Usually, she sat at a desk with academic journals spread out to synthesize what scholars said about medieval mythology. Then she'd look up their sources until she found more articles on law in the Middle Ages, property documents related to women, and so on. But today she was out in the wild chasing down a creature that wasn't exactly myth. The dobhar-chu was mentioned in one of the myths because its pelt was supposedly able to deflect spears. Once she began researching "the Irish Crocodile" — a seven-foot-long cross between a hound and an otter, Rosie read that possessing even one inch of its pelt was able to keep a ship from wrecking, a horse from injury, and a man from wounds from gunshot or any other means. While this all fit within the realm of mythology, the handwritten book Jordan had produced contained what seemed to be first-person accounts of seeing this creature. Rosie didn't know how that would fit into an academic paper, but she had to investigate.

The most famous account was of a woman named Grace Connolly who'd come to the water's edge either to bathe or wash clothes. A number of streams fed the lake from the north while the lake then drained south into the Bonet River. That meant numerous channels with thick reeds and places to hide or get lost. The dobhar-chu leapt from the water and mauled Grace to death. Her husband Terrence found her and horrified, stabbed the creature in the neck with a dagger.

Reaching the end of the path, Rosie took out her phone to snap pictures. Two other people in windbreakers walked past her and then she had a moment alone with the water thundering in her ears and the dark pool swirling. She took an involuntary step back from the edge. It was too easy to feel the predatory teeth of an angry, over-sized otter sinking into her boot, jerking her toward a watery grave. If she'd tried to fight back, the dobhar-chu would whistle for his mate. Calling back-up. She shivered and rubbed away the goosebumps as she started back up the path toward the parking lot.

After reading about this cryptid, Rosie had pulled up videos on YouTube of otter attacks. Not the sweet, small animals that held hands while they floated on their backs, but the otter clans that worked together to harass and distract a caiman for hours until, as a group, they drowned the predator who might have eaten their young. She shoved the phone back in her pocket. There was also the recent report of an otter approaching kayakers and surfers in California. The female pup had been taken away from her mother, her mother killed for being "aggressive," and then the pup released back into the wild. The pup wouldn't leave the area now that humans had fed her. Wildlife officials were now calling the pup "aggressive" in what Rosie considered the first step toward "removal."

More hikers passed Rosie as she emerged from the woods. She walked along the road, following it around a curve until she came to Tourist Information. The building had large windows that let in the natural light and a rack of colorful brochures in front of a large desk. Public restrooms on one side and a snack shop on the other. Rosie approached the desk.

A husky young man with red hair gave her a nod. "Do you need a boating license?"

"No."

"Directions to Manorhamilton Castle?"

"Nope." Rosie didn't wait for more suggestions. "I'm interested in dobhar-chu."

"Ahh." He grinned at her. "There's a sixteen-verse poem that narrates the story pretty clearly, especially the part with the horse, but it's not really in pamphlet form."

She'd read the poem. After Terrence killed the dobhar-chu, its mate had leapt from the water. The man jumped on his horse to ride away, but the creature chased him to the next village. There Terrence and his brother-in-law put their horse in front of an open door and, depending on which version you read, either let the creature go under the horse and chopped off its head or the creature had gone through the horse, getting stuck long enough for them to cut off its head.

"Do you have anything to add?" She leaned forward on the glass and pretended to hold a microphone toward him, "Off the record. Why is the story so popular?"

He laughed, good-natured, and looked around. Customers flowed to and from the snack shop, but no one was in a queue at the information desk.

"I would say the story is well-known because a dobhar-chu is even scarier than a shark." He held up his hand and ticked off reasons on each finger. "Sharks are pre-dinosaur killing machines. So are dobhar-chu. Three types of sharks like human flesh, but all dobhar-chu see humans as prey and, unlike sharks, they seem to enjoy the taste. You escape a shark by getting to land, but dobhar-chu are fast in the water *or* on land. They also mate for life. Very romantic but that means you're messing with a group instead of a loner. Think of Jaws. He didn't have a wife. Or a Jaws Jr. But the dobhar-chu is called "King of the Otters," isn't he? When he whistles, maybe his mate comes or maybe his mate and all their pups." The young man shrugged as he closed his hand into a fist. "They're also migratory. Sure, the story of poor Grace starts here, but many say that the dobhar-chu followed the Irish immigrants right to your own America." He rapped his knuckles against the glass. "Is that what you meant?"

She nodded. Not only had she jotted down what he'd said, but she'd noticed the way that he spoke as if the creature was real. He was quite the storyteller—something she was noticing about so many of the people she'd met in Ireland.

She waved goodbye and headed for her car. Next stop: the cemetery at Conwal.

Growing more confident at navigating, Rosie headed toward the village of Kinlough then pulled into the parking lot by the cemetery. A plaque attached to the front gate announced that many of the graves had been tragically destroyed or lost after World War I. Rosie ran her fingers over the raised letters as if she could connect with deeper meaning in them. Her heart quickened and she dropped her hand to the gate and pushed it open. She was on the trail of a story that couldn't possibly be true—monsters didn't exist—but her research said that both Grace Connolly and her husband Terrence had been buried here.

Rosie moved throughout the uneven rows until she found Grace's marker in the ground. Several flower bouquets were around it. She wondered if they were from locals or tourists. Kneeling in the grass that grew between markers, Rosie squinted at the grave. The slab was so old that most of the details were illegible, but Grace's name and her husband's nickname "Ter" with her death date of "September 24, 1722" were clear. More than that, it had an etching of her killer at the top. The carved image of the dobhar-chu looked like a dog lying down with its head thrown back. Perhaps in its death throes? A knife or spear pierced its neck. Rosie took out her phone and snapped multiple pics. Then she enlarged the image, studying the etching of the human hand that held the end of the weapon and then swiping over to look at the creature's head. This could be the oldest existing artwork of the cryptid. A thought nagged at her, something she was forgetting.

Terrence's gravestone was flat to the ground with grass growing around the edges. No flowers there. She wouldn't have been able to read any of the worn away words, but his also had an etched image: a man riding a horse and holding a dagger in his hand. Taking a step backward, Rosie snapped a photo of the entire graveyard and the mountains in the background. Her boot scraped against the grass as she shifted her weight. Raindrops fell. Was this story a symbol? A cautionary tale? A hoax that had lasted too long? She rubbed at her forehead and thought of the times she'd analyzed how monsters were a reflection of human fears in papers that received high marks. Was this any different? Who was to say that Grace wasn't a victim of domestic abuse and this Terrence made up the entire story, creating an opportunity to become a hero for the next generations. Yet, if she'd learned anything about village life from being on Glenade Island it was that everybody was always watching. It was Mrs. Troutskill who'd pointed out that Peyton was now helping behind the bar at The Sauce while Erika had been Dylan's original pick.

Rain dripped down the collar of her windbreaker. Rosie zipped her phone into a pocket. Man, she really needed that umbrella. She walked back to the car uncertain as to whether today's trip had given her any information that she could use in an academic paper. Slamming the door shut, Rosie shook out her damp hair. Hopefully, the rain would stop in time for the *ceili* tonight. Thunder boomed and lightning cracked across the sky. Rosie turned the windshield wipers to double speed and drove slowly along the route back to the ferry.

Concentrating on the road for so long put an ache in her back right between her shoulder blades and she felt a sense of relief parking next to the construction site. Rosie sighed as she stretched her neck from side to side and then settled back to wait for the ferry. It put her in the perfect position to notice the people huddling under the overhang of the new building. The tall man in the expensive raincoat was definitely Dylan. The other man was older and also wore an expensive coat. That was one thing she'd learned from being married to Kenny and around his family—how to recognize the social mannerisms of money and power. So Dylan pushing a girl with blonde hair in a pink raincoat out into the rain was a power move. Both men watched while the girl struggled through the thick mud to Dylan's car and then brought something back. She held it out to Dylan like an offering before she could step back under the jutting roof. Without thinking too much about it, Rosie took a picture and then enlarged it. Dylan was handing an envelope to the other man. That's what Peyton had fetched from his car.

Rosie looked up in time to see the men shake hands. Then the other man extended an umbrella and walked away toward a black Lexus. After he was gone, Peyton grabbed Dylan's arm and waved with her other hand. It wasn't hard to see that she was complaining about something.

The ferry's foghorn sounded a moment before it appeared, bobbing toward the dock.

Dylan shoved past Peyton and got into his car. Lights illuminated the evening as he turned on the ignition and shifted into drive.

The threat was clear: he was going to leave her if she didn't either agree to whatever he'd said or change her mind about something.

Rosie was already reaching for her door handle—it didn't matter if she liked Peyton or not, no one should be manipulated and threatened—when Peyton ran forward. Her hands touched the hood of the car and then she moved around to the passenger's side and got in. Rosie sat in there while other cars pulled past her onto the ferry. Emotions swirled as memories from times with Kenny ran through her mind.

The foghorn sounded again. Finally, hands shaking, Rosie pulled forward.

Chapter Seven

Driving back onto the island felt like coming home as the rain stopped and a rainbow glowed its beautiful colors overhead. Rosie pushed through the tourist crowds lined up for the ferry and took a deep breath of the distinct air. Maybe it was the sweet smells from the bakery or the scent of hops from the pub or even the extra saltiness from the western wind that swept down from the cliffs. Whatever the recipe was, the combination made Rosie smile.

"Coming to the *ceili* tonight, are you, Rosie?" Dylan stood in front of the pub, Peyton a step behind him.

"Of course," she said, adjusting the strap of her messenger bag. "Midsummer is important in Celtic mythology. I wouldn't miss it for the world. I only hope there will be several bonfires and maybe a pagan offering or two."

"Right." He continued standing there with arms akimbo. "Peyton said she thought she saw your car on the ferry just now."

Rosie looked at the girl, who dropped her eyes in embarrassment. Was she being paranoid or was he asking if she'd seen the rotten way he'd treated Peyton?

"Can't do all my research on the island," she said easily. "Well, I'll see you two later tonight." She gave them a wave and headed toward the spiral stairs, checking the reflection of the cat café to see Dylan watch her for a moment and then turn toward Peyton and give her instructions about what to bring to the *ceili*.

Shrugging off the odd feeling, Rosie hurried up the stairs and opened the door.

"Mom!" Dahlia jumped up from the floor where she was coloring to throw herself at Rosie.

Laughing, Rosie dropped the messenger bag to the ground and enveloped her daughter in a huge hug so that the girl's legs were off the ground.

"I missed you," Dally said, arms around Rosie's neck.

"I missed you too!" Rosie couldn't stop smiling at her daughter. "Wow, who braided your hair? It looks fancy."

"Jordan did."

On a chair between the beds, Jordan lifted her cup of tea in acknowledgement before setting it on the windowsill and moving through the room scooping up the scattered papers covered with Dahlia's drawings.

"What are those?" Rosie asked, adjusting her grip as Dally wrapped her legs around Rosie's waist. "Oof, you're getting too big for this." But Rosie didn't put her down; instead, she pulled gently on the end of Dahlia's braid.

"Jordan and I were playing a game while we waited for you. We were pretending to be different animals on the island and then guessing."

"Fun! May I see the pictures?" Rosie looked at Jordan expectantly.

"It's probably difficult to make out the difference between cats and sheep, at least of my drawings," Jordan said. "I'll just put these in the recycling."

"I insist," Rosie said, holding out her hand. For a moment she thought Jordan was going to ignore her, but then the bookshop manager gave that mysterious half-smile and the little shrug of her shoulders before walking through the door.

She called, "I'm leaving in ten minutes if you want to walk to the *ceili* with me." Then she shut the door before Rosie could answer.

"Perfect." Rosie gave Dahlia one more snuggle and then let her down and set the drawings on the table. "Let Mommy freshen up and then we can go, okay?"

"Okay." Dahlia ran over to sit on the bottom bunk. "I can't wait for the party tonight. Mrs. Troutskill let me help her bake." She giggled. "And then Manny the mule put his head through her window and she let me feed him one of the cookies. Isn't that silly?"

"That is pretty silly," Rosie agreed, searching the closet. Tonight, according to textbooks, would be a festival meant to encourage a year of fertility for the land and its people. She selected a blue maxi dress, kept her boots on, and then grabbed a silk shawl with gold threads. "I'll bring your sweater in my bag."

"I won't get cold. Jordan said there will be a big fire."

"I hope there are marshmallows." Rosie swept the scarf around her shoulders too dramatically. The current caught the coloring pages and scattered them to the floor. "Shoot." She knelt down to pick them up.

A knock at the door signaled Jordan was ready, but shock kept Rosie in place.

"What is this?" she whispered. The last coloring page featured an animal with a long body and duck feet. Whiskers on a face that could be either a dog or an otter. A cross drawn in black on its back. A mouth open with triangle teeth.

"That's the dog I dreamed about." Dahlia didn't seem concerned. She stood next to Rosie to study the picture. "See her duck feet so she can swim fast? And her body goes like this in the water." Dahlia waved her arm like a mermaid swimming. Or, Rosie corrected herself, like a King dobhar-chu. "See those?"

Rosie frowned at the brown squiggly balls in scribbles of green. "Are those toys for the 'dog'?"

Dahlia squealed with laughter.

Jordan knocked again.

"Those are the babies, Mom!" Dahlia grabbed her middle as she bent over, out of breath from laughing. "You thought they were toys."

"The mom has big, pointy teeth," Rosie said. "Maybe she needed something to chew on." That wasn't human, she added silently.

"Those are to keep her babies safe," Dahlia said matter-of-factly. "Grrrrr." She bared her teeth in a growl and put up her hands like claws. "Just like you would do."

Just as Jordan's knocking began again, Rosie wrenched open the door.

"Took you long enough," Jordan said. She wore a sleeveless silk blouse with embroidery around the plunging neckline and tweed trousers. Her violin was strapped to her back.

"Dahlia was explaining this," Rosie said, brandishing the paper with the creature. She searched Jordan's expression to see if the woman felt guilty about telling tales of a monster to a young child or anything else that would explain how Dahlia was dreaming about the dobhar-chu.

"Took you long enough," Jordan repeated. She raised a dark eyebrow. "Shall we go?"

The sun set as they followed the road through the village and up into the hills. Rosie yawned.

"None of that," Jordan admonished. "That's contagious and we have a wild night of frolicking ahead."

"It's been a busy day for me," Rosie protested. Her legs were tired from all the hiking she'd done to the waterfall and around Glenade Lake. "Huh," she said. "I just realized that this island is called Glenade Island, but the lake is on the mainland."

"Glenade Lough is fed by many waterways. It's all connected."

"I see."

They walked around a switchback and, against a darkening sky, a magnificent orangish-red flame licked upward. People moved around, flowing into the open cottage and back into the pasture. Tables and chairs had been set up and it seemed that everyone dropped off a dish to share and then went to explore what Dylan had set up at the outside bar. Peyton stood next to him, dipping into coolers and setting up cups.

"That's so beautiful," Dahlia said, grabbing Rosie's hand and pointing to the bonfire with the other. "And so scary."

"I didn't bring any food," Rosie said. "I'm sorry. I should have picked up something on the mainland."

"That's all right. This is your first one so you're still a guest." Jordan touched the strap of her violin. "Besides, I brought my music and isn't that enough of a gift for everyone?"

"Truly humble," Rosie teased.

As they got closer, Rosie realized how immense the bonfire was. Pallets and logs had been laid crisscross to build a rectangular tower. The whole thing was ablaze. Pops and snaps of sap punctuated the air while a wall of warmth spread from the tower.

"What happens when this collapses?" Rosie asked as she looked around for a hose or other way to extinguish the fire if it got out of control.

"We drive the cattle through the embers, of course." Jordan leaned close to her ear. "Thought you were the mythology expert."

"Mom," Dahlia pulled on her hand. "May I go with the twins to make husk babies?"

"Twins?" Thinking of the Mrs. Troutskills, Rosie glanced around to see two girls around her daughter's age. "Who are they?"

"They're my friends, Mom." Dahlia sighed theatrically. "Francis and Keller are Mrs. Troutskill's granddaughters. We work on the farm together when they don't have school. Our American summer is longer than theirs."

"Ah." Rosie shook her head, bemused. "Of course. Go make husk babies." Watching the three girls dash away, Rosie wondered how she'd missed that Dahlia had made friends. Her quiet little girl was part of a group.

Jordan reappeared with a beer bottle in one hand and a glass of wine in the other. "Here. It's what you had the other night, although you don't seem like a big drinker."

Rosie shook her head but accepted the wine. She hadn't known that Jordan noticed her drink preferences. "I want to have a clear head in case anything goes wrong. Maybe it's a mother thing."

"Na, I know plenty of mothers who will have a nip of something now and then, even stronger than wine. I think it's a response to what you told me about your ex-husband." Jordan tilted the bottle back, her fingers lightly around the neck. "This is the night that worlds clash together. Strange things can happen. Sip that wine, Anne-Rose." She touched her bottle to Rosie's glass. "Sláinte."

"Sláinte," Rosie repeated.

"Na, say 'Sláinte agatsa.' That's the answer."

Rosie nodded. "Sláinte agatsa."

Together they took a drink.

"There you go," Jordan said. "We'll make an islander out of you yet."

The wine tasted good, earthy and complex. Had she eaten today? The sky was full dark now and without any city lights to obscure them, the stars shined. Wind whipped the flames so that they danced as if possessed. There was Ernie who owned the fishing shop. He raised his drink to her in greeting as he went into the house. And Mrs. Troutskill was over getting a drink from Peyton. And other Mrs. Troutskill was over at a table examining the shepherd's pie. Even Dimitri and Erika had shown up. They'd gone straight to Dylan's table.

"What," Rosie said, feeling very bold, "does it take to become an islander? Do I have to be initiated into a secret ritual?"

The firelight caught in Jordan's grey eyes. "I'm sure I don't know anything about that," she said coolly.

"That's not quite true, is it?" Rosie took a swallow of the wine. How was it half gone already? "Everyone here has a secret and I'm tired of it."

Jordan finished her bottle and tossed it into a recycling bin. "You're not exactly straightforward, are you?"

"I am," Rosie declared. "What you see is what you get."

"Even your name isn't your own." Jordan nodded. "At first I thought it was too cute that you were 'Rosie' and she was 'Dahlia' and then I realized they weren't real."

"They are real. They weren't the names we were born with, but we chose them and that makes them even more special." Rosie's chest heaved. "Our secret was to protect us. At least we aren't wandering around in the middle of the night in a field that you told us to stay away from or coming back with blood dripping off our clothes or sending Manny the Mule away even though you know my daughter adores him or—"

"Shhh, now." Jordan covered Rosie's mouth with her hand and then dragged her farther into the pasture away from the bonfire. Rosie would have tripped over the random stones littering the field if Jordan hadn't been supporting her. "Aren't you the observant one?"

She removed her hand, but Rosie could still taste the rose lotion she'd used.

"I wasn't finished." Rosie put her hands on her hips. "You're keeping some secret from me that made my daughter draw a creature from folklore. The same creature I was investigating on the mainland today."

"Is that it?"

"And you didn't tell me that you'd been arrested for illegal entry in an animal cruelty case. But that's in the past so maybe that doesn't count. But it is kind of a lie that you're just a nice bookshop manager and maybe there's a mysterious owner—that's a secret—and you sell flowers. There's more to it than that."

"Are we talking about lies in addition to secrets?" A pale pink flush stained Jordan's cheeks. "Because the biggest lie of all is you saying that you want to be a professor to give Dahlia security, because you'd have to travel around taking whatever short jobs you could trying to get tenure. And you don't want to be a professor because you like lecturing. You already told me that being in the classroom is draining. Na, you want to be a professor because you think that that will make people listen to you. Nobody believed you about your ex-husband. Even your family. But if you can get a 'Doctor' in front of your name then you think it will change everything."

Rosie shook her head. Jordan had no idea what was important in academia.

"Here's the thing, Anne-Rose or whatever your name is. Having a degree isn't going to change anything." Jordan poked her in the chest. "You have to believe in yourself. Grab your confidence and don't let go. Then you'll be brave enough to do what suits you without needing approval."

Tears filled Rosie's eyes and she didn't know why, but she didn't want to wipe them away in case Jordan couldn't tell in the darkness.

Jordan took the wine glass from Rosie's numb hand and tipped it up, finishing the red wine and handing back the empty glass.

"I'm off to play a set. If you want me to tell you my secrets afterward, I will." Jordan stalked through the night; her familiar gait outlined by flames as she walked toward the crowd around the bonfire.

Shaking, Rosie settled into the grass of the pasture and then laid on her back and stared up at the stars while her mind spun. The smell of burning wood from the bonfire competed with the scents of food on the outside tables. Grass tickled her bare arms. Voices rose and fell in a gentle background noise. Rosie's shoulders relaxed and the sudden opening sensation across her chest made her realize she'd been curving inward in a defensive posture. Just a few more minutes here to get herself together and then she'd find Dahlia and they'd go back home.

But where was home? The east coast? The bookstore café? The future city where she'd have a job? She didn't want to consider that Jordan was right, but when she had pictured getting her Ph.D. it was with a sense of triumph because no one thought she could. But it wasn't like there would be anyone in the audience cheering for her. And afterward... she'd chosen not to think about the process of applying to different colleges and interviewing for a small list of jobs compared to a huge list of new professors. And there was no security without tenure so she could potentially be moving Dahlia around from school to school as she looked for an academic community with a niche opening. Comparative mythology wasn't exactly a requirement at universities, but it was what she loved. Today had been so fun. Seeing the actual lake and then taking pictures of the graves. But what was she supposed to do now? And what had Jordan meant that she would share all her secrets?

Violin notes sang into the night.

Rosie sat up and pushed away a sharp rock digging into her leg. Just as she decided to stay here for a private concert, two people came through the darkness arguing.

As they got closer, Rosie tried to sneak away. However, the maxi dress made it difficult to crawl and when the material bunched around her knees, she knocked over the wine glass and it hit the rock she'd just moved. The glass broke into large pieces. Stifling a curse, she began picking up pieces so neither animal nor human would get cut.

"I'm just saying that you've changed since we first got here and I don't like it." That was Dimitri's distinctive voice. "Whenever you're around him you act like a servant. And you constantly wonder if he's mad at you. That's bullshit. Where's the girl who wore the t-shirt claiming she was a Woman-Boss? Because you aren't acting like it. And he's not acting like he cares about you."

Peyton's voice was muffled and she sounded as if she'd been crying. "I know you can't see it, but he really does care about me. He's teaching me a lot about the hospitality industry. And he has to flirt with the tourists—he's charming and that's what gets the tips. It's hard because the island isn't getting enough visitors. He's trying to change that, but no one will listen, so he needs me. I'm what keeps him sane."

"You're what keeps him sane! That's some fucked up gaslighting right there. He's an adult—older than you—and he makes his own decisions. You aren't an emotional support animal. I would never treat a girl like that. Especially if I cared about her."

Rosie sat back on her heels; hands full of glass. Wow. She hadn't really thought that Dimitri was so perceptive.

A slow clapping filled the air and the silhouettes of two more people approached. Erika and Dylan.

Dylan continued clapping as he walked right up to Dimitri. "You deserve an Oscar, bro." He slid an arm around Peyton's shoulders and kissed the top of her head. "I'm not mad at you," he said to her. To Dimitri, he said, "You've been trying to decide whether to lust after Peyton or Erika this whole time and when I hit it off with Peyton you got jealous." Dylan pointed to Erika. "Didn't think about hurting this girl's feelings, did you? Of course she's going to come tell me what you're up to. You messed up, little man. You've revealed yourself and we all see how lame you are."

Rosie's stomach churned. Her head pounded as memories of fights with Kenny surfaced.

Dimitri protested, "Erika, you see that he's manipulative. You agreed that it isn't healthy the way that Peyton reacts to every little thing Dylan wants."

Erika tossed her hair. "That's not Dylan's fault. And I can't believe I let you kiss me. Dylan's right. You're lame."

"Peyton," Dimitri pleaded. "Come on. This is crap. I was looking out for you."

"No, you weren't." She leaned in closer to Dylan. "I'm in love and that makes you jealous."

Dimitri threw his hands into the air so that his gold watch flashed in the bonfire's light. "You know what, you all deserve each other. I'm out."

Music swelled from the cottage's open windows. They were playing some tavern song and Jordan's voice sang out the verse.

Dimitri started to stalk past Rosie, who hunched down even tighter, but Dylan laughed. "You're going the wrong way."

"This is the way we came up," Dimitri argued.

This close, Rosie could smell the alcohol on him. *Please don't get in a physical fight,* she pleaded silently. Even watching this confrontation was bringing back painful memories and her body felt ill.

"It is," Dylan agreed. "But that's the long way. I'll take you to a shortcut. It's steep but will cut your time in half. Follow it and you'll come out in the flower meadow behind the bookstore café." He sounded almost cheerful as he took Dimitri's arm. "Get in bed and sleep it off tonight. You'll feel better."

"Fine."

"Erika, take him over to my table and get him a drink for his walk home."

Once Erika and Dimitri were out of earshot, Dylan gave Peyton a little shake. "I told you not to be alone with him."

"I'm sorry, I didn't mean to. He said he needed to talk to me." Peyton said. "Ouch! You're hurting me. Let me go, please."

"Do you want me to let you go? Stop letting you help behind the bar? Stop teaching you how to be a bartender?" Dylan released her shoulders and then gave her a push. "Because I'm about to make it big and if you don't want to be part of it, that's fine."

"Dylan, I'm sorry." She ran forward and pressed herself up against his chest, lifting her face for a kiss, but he just stared. "Please, baby. I won't do it again."

Slowly he enveloped her in a hug and rocked back and forth. His accent came out strong as he said, "There, now, there's my girl. Don't test me like that again. You make me do things."

"I won't." She sounded so grateful. "I'll be good."

"That's what I want to hear." His voice was a soft croon. "Let's go direct our friend Dimitri to the Queen's Church."

They walked away together, holding hands.

Rosie's stomach flipped and she vomited into the grass. Her hands were wet and sticky, and she couldn't catch her breath. Her phone was in her purse, she needed it for the flashlight, but her stomach cramped again, and she threw up.

Finally, overcome, she rolled onto her side, brought her legs into fetal position, and closed her eyes.

Chapter Eight

"Hells! I almost tripped over you."

Gentle hands eased Rosie into a seated position. Her mouth tasted sour, and her hands stung. Still dazed, Rosie glanced toward the bonfire and saw that several smaller fires had sprung up in each of the cardinal directions.

"Anne-Rose." Jordan's firm voice cut through the fog. "Can you get up?" Light flared from her phone. "Bloody hell! What did you do to your hands?"

Rosie licked her lips and shuddered. "The wine glass," she whispered. She'd been holding the broken pieces while being forced to listen to Dylan talking to Peyton. Kenny had spoken to her the same way, and like Peyton, she hadn't fought back. Instead, she'd believed him, lost all self-confidence, and changed anything and everything so he wouldn't get mad.

"I see that. I guess I'll ditch my speech about how you should have been listening to our music and dancing on Midsummer instead of hiding in the pasture." Jordan squatted down and plucked the pieces of glass out of Rosie's bleeding hands and from the grass. "I'm going to wrap them in your scarf—thoughtful of you to wear that in case this happened—and get you inside so I can clean up your hands. Dally's asleep in the window seat of the cottage, so you don't need to worry about her."

Rosie leaned against Jordan, palms tucked to her chest, as they worked their way through the pasture and then past people sitting in outside chairs smoking pipes or telling stories. Others had spread out blankets and were either sleeping or stargazing. Teenagers ran through the seated adults, playing some type of game and wearing painted masks. The closest teen's mask was red with horns on either side. Rosie squinted, clutching Jordan's arm. She felt disoriented, swirling like the stars overhead, somehow invisible as she walked through the Irish crowd on this pagan night.

Then Jordan pushed her into the cottage and through the living room. She caught sight of Dahlia curled in the window seat with a blanket draped over her, just like Jordan said. The room smelled like vanilla and cinnamon and chocolate all at once. A moment later they moved through a kitchen packed with desserts of every type. Three women with white hair watched them curiously, but Jordan kept pushing Rosie until they were in a small laundry room.

"A bit of privacy here and, if I remember correctly, a First Aid kit as well." Jordan pushed Rosie toward the sink and searched the cabinets until she produced the kit. Setting it aside, she turned the knobs and tested the water. "All right, let's rinse you off."

The water turned pink when it ran over her hands and Rosie looked away, inhaling in pain as Jordan patted her hands dry.

"Are you ready to tell me what happened?" Jordan guided her to sit on an upside-down laundry basket and then squatted down so they were eye-level.

How could she explain? It would sound silly to say that watching someone else's fight had brought up her past trauma and she'd acted like a baby, accidentally clutching pieces of glass in her fists and puking up half a glass of wine because she hadn't had anything to eat. She was such an idiot.

"Hey!" Jordan lifted her chin. "I don't know what is going on in your head, but I don't like it."

"I'm sorry," Rosie said, unthinking, and then winced. Apologizing like Peyton. Apologizing the way she used to.

"Nothing to be sorry about. And you don't have to tell me if you don't want to." Jordan took Rosie's hands in her own and turned them back and forth. "The cuts don't look deep enough to need stiches, but you're going to have scars on your palms." She took gauze from the kit and began wrapping the white material around Rosie's hands.

"It will be hard for a palm reader to tell my fortune," Rosie joked.

"We make our own fortune," Jordan said briskly. "Want to see my scar?"

Surprised, Rosie met Jordan's grey eyes. Such a personal invitation. Jordan always looked like a bored model and here she was offering to be vulnerable, to show her imperfection.

"Yes," Rosie whispered.

"Okay," Jordan agreed, but she stayed in the squat as if maybe she hadn't meant to make the offer. Abruptly, the black-haired woman stood and pulled up the leg of her pants. Above her knee was a pink scar of mangled flesh, long healed. A bite. Something with sharp teeth had bitten deep into the flesh and hadn't wanted to let go. Had maybe even eaten a piece of Jordan.

Eyes wide, Rosie shook her head. So many questions. All she managed was, "Are you okay?"

Jordan snorted as she dropped the pants leg back into place. "Of course I'm not okay. The dobhar-chu bit me, would have killed me, and then had to be put down because it tasted human flesh. They become obsessed and will hunt humans across land and through water. So it was an absolute mess of a rescue."

"Dobhar-chu?" Rosie repeated, not quite understanding. Laughter floated in through the open window. Was Jordan telling a story? Was this a joke to play off what happened to her leg?

"Well now, here's the thing. I'm a cryptid keeper. We rescue, remove, and rehome cryptids." She smoothed back her hair in what would have been a nervous gesture if anyone besides Jordan Rooney had done it. "That was my first recovery mission after Saoirse recruited me." Giving one of her trademark shoulder shrugs, Jordan added, "It was in Baltimore's Inner Harbor. That's why I have that postcard on the café's bulletin board. I'll tell you the full story another time when we aren't crammed in a laundry room."

Rosie shook her head. "Dobhar-chu are real? Why would you keep that a secret?" She stood up in the tiny room and paced back and forth. "Can you imagine how exciting it would be for the world to find out that this ancient species is not only real, but still alive?"

"That's exactly why we keep them a secret." Jordan squeezed against the wall to make room for Rosie's pacing. "I told you that I always put animals first. People are stupid. I'm not angry about being bitten. That was the dobhar-chu's nature. But humans will come here to see our cryptids and then chase them down to get selfies. Tourists will stalk the babies."

"Babies?" Rosie thought of the picture that Dahlia had drawn. The brown blobs hiding in high grass.

"Imagine a sweet otter pup mixed with a retriever puppy. Who wouldn't want to cuddle that? It's like what they do to tigers: locking them in cages, breeding them, taking their babies, selling photos to the humans holding the babies, and then murdering those babies when they are older because the meat they need to live is too expensive."

Rosie's stomach clenched. She could picture the abuse that Jordan cited.

"Even if we prevent zoos from stealing our dhobar-chu, tourists will come here and throw food so they can see a real-life cryptid. Then the animals get addicted. It's a lot easier to approach tourists for food than to stalk your own. Think of the bears in America's national parks. Humans feed the bears or leave out food and it's the animal that gets put down."

Closing her eyes, Rosie nodded.

"Finally, there will be at least one person who wants to "battle" the cryptid—either to have a trophy for their wall, for their own story, or to film it and make themselves famous for being an asshole. Tell me I'm wrong."

She couldn't. Jordan and her friends had obviously thought this through and keeping the dobhar-chu a secret was the best option for the animals. "That's why you don't want more tourists on the island."

"The more humans there are, the most chance of discovery. And the queen's been acting up lately."

"The queen? I thought the leader was a King Otter?"

"Patriarchal mistake. The leader of the pack is the mama until one of her daughters challenges and kills her."

There wasn't enough air in the laundry room for Rosie to breathe. Jordan was speaking so matter-of-factly about something that couldn't possibly be true, but all the clues aligned. She still had a question, though.

"What do you mean that the queen is acting up? Why was your cloak bloody? Did she attack you?"

"May I get another beer?" Jordan made a show of stretching. "This could take a while."

"In a minute." Rosie sat back down on the laundry basket. "Talk."

Jordan let out a big breath. "I think someone's been deliberately feeding the dobhar-chu to lure them out from their area. This person, whoever it is, wants the cryptids to be seen."

Acid swished around in Rosie's stomach. She had a pretty good idea who it was. And it would explain why he'd been buying more fresh meat from Mrs. Troutskill.

A sudden banging on the door made them both jump.

"MOMMY!"

Rosie leapt forward and then cried out when her bandaged hands hit the knob. Jordan was right behind and pushed Rosie out of the way to open the door.

"You're a terrible patient," Jordan scolded.

Dahlia's eyes were wide with fear, her expression offset by a Midsummer painted mask. "They said your hands were bleeding and I couldn't find you."

"I'm okay. I got a couple of cuts, but I'm all bandaged now." Rosie held up her hands, aware that the bandages made her look like she was wearing white oven mitts. "See?"

Dahlia's mouth trembled and she pulled at the hem of her shirt. To distract her, Rosie said, "I like your face painting. Who did that?" Half of Dally's face was painted like a porcelain doll with glitter swept across her cheekbone.

"A woman with white hair. She's Mr. Ernie's sister or something and then Keller came over and she said that you were almost fainting, and Ms. Jordan had to carry you and blood was everywhere."

"That's not quite accurate," Rosie said. "But you can see I'm all right and I need to talk for one more minute and then we can go back to the loft. This Midsummer was quite exciting."

"My head hurts. Can I just stay with you? I don't want to be around any of the kids anymore." Dahlia squeezed onto the floor and wrapped her arms around her knees. "I'm worried about you."

"I'll leave you two alone," Jordan said, moving toward the door. "Be careful with those hands."

"Jordan," Rosie called. "The thing you told me... I think you're right and I might know who it is and... we have a very big problem."

Jordan stared at her and, without breaking eye contact, shut the door again.

Cutting her eyes to Dahlia and then back, "If there was a community of alligators on the island, where would they be?"

"This island is volcanic. There's a system of tunnels underneath the island between the western cliff where the keeper's house is—do you know?"

Rosie nodded, thinking of the carved dobhar-chu on the wall.

"And the northeastern part of the island where no one lives, back in the forest behind my café."

Yes, that's exactly what she'd thought. "And all the islanders know about the… alligators."

"Same as they all know about the cuts on your hands. Maybe embellished. Maybe some details are rearranged. But, yes, it's what we call an open secret."

"And does the phrase "the Queen's Church" mean anything to you?"

Jordan frowned. "Who else have you been talking to?"

"Dylan. He said he would show Dimitri a shortcut to the Queen's Church."

"Dylan? He's a fool. Not even an islander." Jordan rubbed a hand across her face. "When is he going to do that? A field trip tomorrow with their phones out? At the weekend? I'm going to explain exactly why that is a bad idea. And then I will smash their phones if they decide not to listen to me being reasonable."

Rosie turned her bandaged hands back and forth. Dimitri could be in trouble right now, stumbling through the dobhar-chu's territory and it was her fault for not saying something sooner.

No. She wasn't going to hold herself responsible for everyone's mistakes. It was Dylan's fault if he'd chosen to put Dimitri in danger and expose the cryptids. She straightened her shoulders. Not her fault, but she could decide to help.

"He already did."

Jordan's typical bored expression was replaced by a series of emotions: surprise, distress, anger, and then her eyes narrowed, and she ripped open the laundry room door. Rosie would have enjoyed seeing Jordan get emotional if the situation hadn't been so dire. As it was, she ran after the cryptid keeper with Dally trailing after her.

"Where are you going?" Rosie called, which was ridiculous because she knew where Jordan was going, but she needed to make the woman stop so they could put together a plan.

"Mom," Dally called. "Don't leave me."

Rosie stopped at the doorway between the kitchen and living room. Jordan had scooped up her violin and settled the strap over her shoulder. She was smiling as she hugged Mrs. Troutskill and thanked her for her hospitality. Beyond the windows, the bonfire had burned down to an orange glowing pile and the other fires were almost out. Rosie, holding Dally's hand, stepped next to Jordan and added her gratitude for hosting Midsummer.

"The shortest night of the year is coming to an end." Mrs. Troutskill nodded. "Enjoy your new beginnings, girls. As for me, I'm about to take a turn dancing."

They followed her outside where the party's energy had picked up. Two of the musicians played, drinks flowed, and Mrs. Troutskill was right: people danced either as couples or alone.

Jordan veered to the left and Rosie trotted behind until they were away from the crowd. Jordan abruptly pivoted. "Have I made a terrible choice to tell you all this? Because I don't have time to waste if I'm going to fix—"

"Are you asking if I'm scared by a bevy of ancient monsters living in the ocean dreaming about human blood?"

"No. I'm asking if you are going to betray that bevy for a shot at your dream of becoming a famous professor and write an academic paper that will send so-called experts to destroy our island and our animals." Jordan's chest heaved. "Don't answer. I don't want any lies between us."

Rosie's mouth dropped open at the unfairness. Dylan was the one trying to betray the island's secret. What had she done to signal that she'd write about cryptids and how would Rosie's lie be worse?

"Why," Rosie challenged. "Are we friends?"

Dally spoke up, "I don't want you to hurt the mama," she made finger quotes, "'alligator.' She's just like us."

Jordan's gaze dropped to Dahlia. "Why do you say that?"

"She wants to protect her babies. Mom always says that she'll do anything for me. This mama's just the same."

"Hmmm." Jordan looked out over the tree line and rubbed at her leg. In the distance, the horizon had a slight lightening. "I'll keep that in mind, little Dally. Now you two go back to the party. It's understood that people will fall asleep wherever they can find a spot."

Rosie stared at Jordan's leg. That's why she wanted to fix what Dylan had done. This was Jordan's shot at redemption for the dobhar-chu who'd had to be put down from biting her.

"No. It's too dangerous," Jordan said.

"I didn't even say anything."

"Your face shows every thought inside your head."

Rosie lifted her chin. "Dimitri was drinking, and it was dark. He probably wandered off the path and curled up to sleep until morning. And the more people who look, the faster we'll find him."

"Fine, but I'm not responsible for your choices. You're a grown woman." Jordan set off through the trees.

"You're not leaving me," Dally said, hands on hips. "I know what the mama is thinking. I dream about her all the time. And if you leave me here, I'll run after you."

Rosie looked from Dally to Jordan's retreating back.

"I promise that I'll be careful," Dally said. Then she opened her bookbag. "Besides, I'm the only one who thought to grab cupcakes for our snack when I went through the kitchen."

"I'm going to ground you for this," Rosie muttered, grabbing Dahlia's hand and running after Jordan into the Queen's Church.

Chapter Nine

The air hung heavy as they walked through the forest, sweeping the light from their phones side to side.

"You still haven't explained your cloak," Rosie said, finally.

"The meadow behind the café is a buffer. Periodically, I go out to make sure that nothing has crossed over the creek. Soon after you first arrived, I found a half-eaten carcass of a buck." Jordan glanced at Dally to make sure that wasn't too graphic. "It was halfway between the nave of Queen's Church and the creek."

The buck she'd seen the first morning? Rosie shivered. This dohbar-chu was a killer, driven by instinct and she had to remember that. Would its sharp teeth have clamped on the buck's leg? Its neck muscles tensed as it shook the prey?

"The problem was, the next time I went out the carcass had been moved. Not closer to the nave, which would make sense for feeding the community, but closer to the meadow."

"They are territorial animals," Rosie said, putting the pieces together. "Dylan was trying to break the boundary so they would believe more of the island was theirs to roam."

"Even worse, he'd stuffed extra hunks of beef inside the buck's carcass so that it would smell fresh. More enticing. He must have poured a bucket of blood on top for good measure. Mrs. Troutskill will be mad when she goes to make blood sausage and her main ingredient has gone missing." She shrugged. "I grabbed the buck's leg, but then the beef fell out so I had to use my cloak underneath the carcass and drag the whole thing closer to the nave."

Rosie could picture it—the dark figure working under the cover of night to undo the situation that Dylan had selfishly created. "I'm sorry you had to do it by yourself."

Surprised, Jordan glanced over. "Thanks." She turned off the flashlight on her phone and Rosie realized that more of the sky had lightened, and the trees had thinned as they moved toward the coast. They were on the eastern side of the island, north of the village. "We're approaching the nave. Hopefully, that means that Dimitri managed to stumble through the woods and make it back to his hotel room where he is sleeping off a massive hangover and this was all for nothing."

"I brought cupcakes," Dally offered.

"Help!" A man's panicked cry rang out through the forest. Dimitri. "Help! I'm lost."

"Of course," Jordan said, rolling her eyes. "He would be at the nave." She took off at a run.

Rosie and Dally sprinted after her.

"What's a nave?" Dally asked as they slowed down to navigate a slight drop-off to the beach. Ahead, Dimitri knelt in the sand next to a large piece of driftwood while Jordan exhorted him to get up.

"The central part of a church," Rosie said, helping her daughter clamber down. "I'm not sure why they call this — oh."

Rocks had formed a half-cave to the right — a natural barrier between this part of the coast and the harbor. Overhead, the rock wall curved like the roof of a cathedral. While they watched, the sun rose against a glorious background of pink and peach hues, emerging from the horizon line like an ancient sun deity on the day after Midsummer. The beauty washed away everything for a moment — all of Rosie's fear, and her aching hands, and the strange night that had just finished. Peace filled her as the sound of lapping waves and the smell of saltwater surrounded them.

"Rosie?" Jordan called in a low voice. "We need to get out of here. This is exactly the wrong place to be."

Rosie blinked. *Right. Ancient monsters.*

Dimitri was up but wandering around muttering about how he'd lost his phone.

"Did someone make this?" Dally asked.

Jordan walked over to her, and Rosie joined them. Right in the center of the "floor" of the half-cave was a rough rectangle shape about the size of a queen-sized bed. Dark water lapped against the edges of the rock.

"The nave is natural, as far as anyone knows," Jordan whispered. "It is also the mouth of the tunnel that leads underneath the island. Not a fun place to play."

The water in the nave splashed farther, wetting another section of rock. Again, the water splashed—no longer a pattern mimicking waves hitting shore, but a signal that something was coming.

"Get back," Jordan said, eyes wide. "Don't run—that's what prey does—but back away toward the meadow. We aren't far. The boundary of the creek should hold."

Rosie, mother's instinct roaring, had already grabbed Dally. They stared at the nave as they walked backward over the sand toward the trees that were part of the forest abutting the meadow, Rosie's arm across Dally's chest like a seatbelt in a car.

Jordan backed away as well, but she'd slung her violin case across her chest.

Rosie's feet hit a root. They'd made it to the woods. Then she saw Dimitri. He was still on the beach near the driftwood.

"Dimitri!" Rosie whispered in her teacher's voice. "Come over here now."

He blinked and then stood up, waving when he saw them. "Hey, I'm glad to see you," he said, as if they hadn't already found him. "I lost my phone and didn't know where I was."

Dally and Rosie made frantic hurry-up gestures while Jordan stood guard, halfway between the nave and the woods, her violin in her hands.

Then, the water from the nave gushed and dark, wet bodies poured out.

"Ohhhh," Dally let out a long breath.

Rosie didn't blame her. The dobhar-chu pups were heartbreakingly cute. They had the long bodies of otters and the faces of a sweet retriever, and they tumbled over each other as they ran around the beach smelling everything.

"NO!" Jordan said, but it was too late.

Dimitri caught sight of the pups and immediately fell to his knees. The pups rushed over—it was difficult to count but Rosie thought either six or seven of them—and sniffed at Dimitri's fingers, at his legs.

"The queen is coming," Jordan shouted at him. "If she bites you then she'll become fixated. Your life is in danger."

He laughed as they crawled over him, their little webbed feet pushing against his back.

"Those pups are wild, Dimitri," Jordan tried again. "They aren't sophisticated, but they are a community of predators."

"That tickles," Dimitri said, scrunching his head down to protect his neck. "Ow! Stop it. Their teeth are sharp." He twisted and squirmed under the mass of bodies. "They're biting me! It hurts." He pushed one away, but then two more took its place.

The pups seemed to think it was a game. The fabric on his pants ripped. Dimitri rolled around on the sand, covering his head with his hands and kicking his legs. "Get them off of me," he cried.

Jordan shook her head as she looked at Rosie.

Any second the pups were going to break Dimitri's skin with their sharp teeth and this would turn from a game into a feeding frenzy.

"I have cupcakes," Dally said. She yanked the zipper on her bookbag and pulled out the napkin-wrapped sweets. Holding one in each hand, Dally whistled.

The whistle got the pups' attention, and several stopped, paws continuing to push Dimitri down, but their faces in the air to sniff for food or danger.

Dally waved the cupcakes in the air.

"Good idea," Jordan said, "but they aren't going to be attracted to sugar and vanilla." She strode forward. "Dimitri—roll your body across the sand to the driftwood. I'll scoop out a hole and you can hide underneath."

And then what? The dobhar-chu's webbed feet would dig faster than Jordan's human hands.

Rosie unwrapped the gauze around her hands. A shark could smell a drop of blood in the water from a quarter of a mile away. Let's see if the dobhar-chu can compete with that.

"Mom, what are you doing?"

"You had the right idea about food," Rosie said. "Give me the cupcakes. Now, stay here and get ready to back away again."

Rosie moved purposefully to the nave. Two of the pups stopped nipping Dimitri to watch her. Setting the cupcakes down on the beach, she clenched her fists. The cuts ripped open again. Rosie let drops of blood from her left hand fall onto the cupcakes. Unsure if it would work, or how much was needed, she then stepped to the nave and held her left hand over the lapping water. Rosie deliberately pulled apart the ripped skin so that red blood ran down the tips of her fingers to fall into the dark water.

The pups tumbled off Dimitri to investigate the cupcakes.

Jordan hurried forward to help the man up. His shirt and pants hung in shreds from the pup's nails and holes in the cloth showed where they had bitten. His hair was sandy and tousled, his shoes were missing, and the flesh of his cheek was swollen, but didn't look like any skin had been punctured.

Rosie turned him around and helped him cross the sand toward where Dally waited.

She waved to her daughter, a signal to go, and Dally nodded. She cupped her hands over her mouth and called. "The Mama-alligator is coming." Then she pivoted and obeyed. Her bright backpack disappeared as she jogged toward the meadow.

"They weren't dogs," Dimitri whimpered. "Or otters. They were horrible."

"I know, but you shouldn't have been here," Rosie soothed. "This is *their* territory."

"You're blaming me?" Dimitri's wide eyes got even wider. "How was I supposed to know?"

They had drawn even with the nave and Jordan was right behind them, but the pups had finished the bloody cupcakes. Could they still smell her hands? Would they dogpile on her the way they had Dimitri?

Water slapped against the rock edges of the nave.

An orange paw emerged from the water. Then a second. With a whoosh of water, a giant white-furred dobhar-chu erupted from the nave. The queen had a black cross on her back and bright orange feet. She lifted her head and gave a series of short, harsh barks.

The pups came to attention and barked back.

Rosie saw the queen's indecision: attack the intruders or check her babies. The queen chose. She was fast, slithering almost, as she flowed from the nave down to the sand. Then she lifted her head to whistle for other adults to come. The guards would be her attack.

But Jordan's bow and fiddle were already up.

As the whistle started, Jordan's music sang its own tune and drowned out the queen's call.

Rosie shoved Dimitri toward the woods as her own mother's instinct insisted she find Dally. "We'll meet in the meadow and figure out what to do. I don't know if they'll be attracted to me because of those cupcakes or not."

Jordan continued to play as she backed away. Rosie moved forward to grab her elbow and guide her over the step into the woods.

The queen watched them, while she dragged each pup over to sniff and examine before reaching for another.

Once they were around the bend in the woods, Jordan used her bow arm to wipe her forehead. "We'll need to hear if she whistles. It won't help much because they are faster than any human, but at least we'll have a warning."

Less than ten minutes later, they'd reached the creek. Dally was standing by the door to the café, nervously twisting the cloth of her shirt. She let out a happy sound when Rosie emerged.

"Hey." Jordan grabbed Dimitri's elbow. "Let's go into the café and talk about what happened."

"Stay away from me," shouted Dimitri, eyes wild, as he sloshed through the creek. "You're all crazy and I'm calling the police or whatever they call them in this rotten country."

Chapter Ten

The islanders, those who'd recovered from Midsummer, gathered on Main Street with an eye toward the ferry. Dylan, excited, practically rubbed his hands together while bouncing on the balls of his feet in front of the closed pub. Peyton stood near him, arms crossed and eyes downcast. Mr. Ernie had come down from the party looking exhausted and set up a folding chair outside his fishing shop, but his sister had stayed behind. Dimitri, standing near his packed luggage, had changed clothes, but his face was still swollen. He ignored everyone and tapped his foot with impatience. Inside the café, Mrs. Troutskill and Jordan sat at the counter sipping lattes and watching the street through the cats' play yard. Dahlia had fallen asleep as soon as she'd gotten out of the shower and assured Rosie that the "mama" wasn't mad.

"She likes that we left. It makes her feel proud." Over-active imagination or total empathy with animals, Rosie wasn't sure. So she just nodded her head and kissed Dally's forehead.

Jordan sighed. "Will you please stop pacing? You're making me tired."

Rosie held up her rewrapped hands and then dropped them. "He's about to spill your island's secret. Tourists will flock here. Dylan will have as much business as he wants and your dobhar-chu will be hunted down and put in zoos."

"Oh, child. Do you think this is the first time we've done this?" Mrs. Troutskill chuckled. "That poor American boy got all turned around on an Irish Midsummer. He drank too much and now he's telling wild tales."

"Why should the police believe you over Dimitri?" Rosie asked.

"It's the whole island, isn't it?" Mrs. Troutskill looked over her mug at Rosie as she took a sip.

"Is it?" Jordan asked pointedly.

Rosie shook her head and walked out of the café.

The ferry's foghorn sounded and both Dimitri and Dylan moved briskly toward the harbor.

Taking the opportunity, Rosie stepped up to Peyton. "We need to talk."

Peyton looked up with tears in her eyes and nodded. They went to the empty lobby of the hotel next door and sank into the padded chairs.

"I don't know what is going on," Peyton said. "Dimitri said that Dylan tried to kill him by sending him into some kind of monster's lair. That makes no sense, but you should have seen him when he came in here this morning to wake me up. He needed my cell phone to call the police. I was afraid Dylan was going to be mad, but he seemed happy."

"Yeah," Rosie nodded. "I would have thought that Dylan would be scared of the police too." She handed Peyton a tissue.

Peyton blew her nose and then went over to the trash station to wipe her hands with sanitizer. "You know about... the mainland?"

Rosie's mind clicked as she synthesized. "The new resort? Yes."

Settling back into the chair, Peyton let out a huge sigh. "I just did what Dylan said, but now I'm freaking out. Am I an accessory to fraud? Or bribery? I'm supposed to be here to learn about hotel management and if this gets out, I could be banned from the business and not get credit for grad school and my parents are going to kill me." Tears filled Peyton's eyes and she seemed to just collapse, hands over her face, as giant sobs shook her slender frame.

Sympathetic tears filled Rosie's eyes, but she made herself stay calm. "Tell me exactly what happened."

"Dylan told me to get cash out of the pub's drawer. The resort is having trouble because a permit got turned down twice. So we went over to meet the inspector to make sure it passed."

"And in return Dylan would have a special relationship with the resort?"

"Yes, he said it would be a great step for my career to be involved in this project and that the island was about to become a tourist attraction and the resort would be the best place to stay."

They watched through the hotel window as two officers walked down Main Street. Dylan gestured to the pub, and they nodded, apparently deciding to use the space for their questioning area. The taller officer shut the door in Dylan's face when he tried to follow inside.

"You knew it wasn't right, but you did it anyway." Rosie made sure that she didn't raise her voice. She was stating facts.

"I thought he loved me." Peyton stood up to gaze out the window while the female police officer waved Dimitri inside the pub. Apparently the questioning had begun.

"Did you?" Rosie asked gently.

"Yes, I..." Peyton swallowed. "At least, I thought he had picked me. Maybe not love, but he thought I would be a good business partner and maybe a romantic summer fling. We would enjoy each other."

Rosie's heart ached because she knew what was coming next. "But he didn't see you that way."

"He slept with Erika last night." Peyton fell back into the chair and squeezed her eyelids closed, but tears leaked out. "You must think I'm so stupid."

"I don't," Rosie said quickly. "And I believe that he used you on purpose."

"You believe me," Peyton said bitterly. "But no one else will. They all think he's so smooth and charming and they think I'm a dumb American slut."

Rosie offered tissues again. "You can regret you decision, but don't call yourself names. We all make mistakes."

Lowering the tissues, Peyton shook her head. "Why are you being so nice to me?"

Outside, Dimitri emerged onto the street and Mrs. Troutskill pushed in front of Mr. Ernie to take her turn inside the pub.

"Yeah, you weren't very nice to me when we first met."

Embarrassed, Peyton looked away.

"But I've been where you are. And it's not great." Rosie licked her lips. "Dylan is not going to change. He'll say he's sorry. He'll buy you things, maybe, or be sentimental. Whatever makes you feel like no one else in the world could know or love you better. And then he'll hurt you, exploit your vulnerabilities, and make you believe it's your fault." She held up her bandaged hands. "That's it. That's the pattern. It doesn't change."

"I don't want that." Peyton's chest heaved.

"Then you have to be strong enough to tell the police what happened between Dylan and the permit inspector. Don't try to spin it. Tell them everything. And then you need to leave this island and not look back." Rosie leaned closer. "The decision you make right now is going to affect the rest of your life."

Rosie patted Peyton's arm and exited the hotel just as Mrs. Troutskill came out of the pub saying, "And don't be a stranger, then" to the female officer. "She's got a second cousin who lived on the island," Mrs. Troutskill informed Rosie.

"You ready?" the officer asked.

"Sure." Rosie looked down at her bandaged hands. *Embrace new beginnings.*

"Mind if I go first?" Peyton gave her hair a little flip.

Rosie stepped aside and gestured Peyton ahead of her. She went up the spiral stairs and waited outside the apartment door, so she'd be close in case Dahlia had a night terror, but she rather thought those were finished.

Hours later, after all the interviews had been taken, the ferry's foghorn summoned tourists to a trip home. Dimitri carried one bag and pulled the one on wheels. Mr. Ernie offered him help but Dimitri kept walking.

The two officers finally emerged with Dylan in handcuffs.

The townspeople watched without even bothering to hide it. Mrs. Troutskill and Mrs. Troutskill had set up chairs on Main Street and one was crocheting while the other knitted.

"Guess that means there's no supper at the pub tonight," Rosie said, following Dally down the stairs.

"You can have an old pastry from the breakfast case," Jordan offered from the café doorway.

"Dahlia might need a little more than that." Rosie smiled as her daughter went straight past Jordan into the cats' playground. "Mind if I use your kitchen to make us some eggs?"

"Sure." Jordan followed Rosie and took a seat while Rosie rummaged for a skillet and spatula. "Did you tell?"

"No."

"Why not?" Jordan pushed black hair behind an ear. "Afraid that your ex-husband will find you when you become an internationally renowned historian?"

Rosie thought of the white dobhar-chu who'd checked her pups first instead of attacking. "Because I understand what the queen wants.

She's not civilized. She's certainly not nice, but I understand her instinct to protect her pups. The police, or animal control, or any humans who think they know best would kill her for attacking a human. But they don't care that Dimitri was in their habitat. Or that Dylan was manipulating them with meat. So maybe I'll finish my paper on Celtic mythology or maybe I won't, but it won't be on the dobhar-chu."

Rosie cracked the eggs into a bowl and set the shells aside. She knew the islanders used shells in everything from plant fertilizer to chicken feed.

"You should have run with Dally as soon as the pups appeared." Jordan tapped a spoon on the counter. "I've fought a dobhar-chu before and you had no experience. Bleeding all over the cupcakes? Dropping blood in the queen's nave? Dimitri was right when he said you were crazy."

"And you played your fiddle to drown out her whistle."

Jordan rolled her eyes.

"I wanted everyone to make it out of the situation alive." She sprinkled in cheese, ham, and diced tomatoes. "All it took was a little of my O+ blood."

"Stop being a martyr, Anne-Rose. You were very brave."

"Call me Rosie." She stirred the eggs and then opened a cabinet to find plates. "All my friends do."

"Stop being a martyr, Rosie, or this isn't going to work. I have to know that you'll take your own life seriously. You lived through your husband, now you live through being a mother. I need you to live for yourself."

"Like what?" Rosie grinned at her. "A cryptid keeper who knows the truth but can't tell the public?"

"Would that be so terrible?"

Rosie turned to face the stove, not ready to consider that Jordan was serious. "Does it pay well? Do I get summers off?" She pivoted to slide a plate in front of Jordan. "Dally! Come eat."

"Not really. It'll be time consuming and frustrating, but you'll be keeping cryptids safe. And you get to travel and see things that the public doesn't. For example, I'll take you to see the Book of Kells this weekend."

Rosie forked a bite of eggs into her mouth. "Pretty sure you have to have a ticket way in advance."

"Maybe for the one on display. Don't you want to see the real one?" Jordan gave her trademark shrug. "What? I know the curator at King's College. We rescued a kelpie together."

About the Author

Sherri Cook Woosley earned an M.A. in English with a focus on comparative mythology from University of Maryland. She also taught Introduction to Academic Writing, Introduction to World Mythology, and Introduction to Folklore at University of Maryland. She's a member of the Science Fiction and Fantasy Writers Association and has published both novels and short stories. Her first children's book *Postcards from a City of Monsters* is forthcoming from Improbable Press. She lives north of Baltimore with her family and various animals and teaches goat yoga to relax. www.tasteofsherri.com.

artist's rendition of Dobhar-Chu

Dobhar-Chú

(Also known as Water Dog, Water Hound, Sea Dog, Irish Crocodile, King of Otters, Father of Otters, dobarcu, doyarchu, dhuragoo, dorraghow, or anchu.)

ORIGINS: The first documented account of this creature in Ireland was in 1722 at Glenade Lough, near the town Creevelea. Oral tradition, however, speaks of tales going back to ancient times. More modern sightings have been reported on Achill Island, west of County Mayo, Omey Island in Connemara, and near Portumna in County Galway.

DESCRIPTION: As with the common otter, the dobhar-chú is partial to the water, found near lakes, rivers, coasts, and waterways of Ireland. Though similar in appearance to its smaller relative, with an elongated neck and sleek, lean body, the dobhar-chú can be between seven and fifteen feet in length. It is said to have some doglike features, while other accounts claim it is actually half dog and half fish. Accounts vary, some saying that it has a dark pelt, and others, a white pelt with black-tipped ears and a shape like a black cross on its back. It is also said to have orange flipper-like feet that are extensively webbed. It is capable of great speeds on land and in the water, and is said to be blood-thirsty and territorial, with a taste for human flesh.

By some folkloric accounts, there is a variation of the dobhar-chú with a long horn on its head. Those who have witnessed this creature report vocalizations of an unusual hissing sound, and also a haunting screech.

In some encounters, it has been said that the dobhar-chú has been accompanied by as many as one hundred conventional otters, which has garnered it the title of King, or Father, of Otters.

Lore and legend claim that this creature's fur is magical, with the power to protect the bearer from harm.

Some theorize this beastie is related to the prehistoric *Siamogale melilutra*, which dates to over six million years ago, was purportedly the size of a wolf, and weighed over one hundred pounds. Or perhaps the *Enhydriodon dikikae*, another gigantic prehistoric creature known as the bear otter.

LIFE CYCLE: The dobhar-chú live as mated pairs and are known to attack in groups of two or more. No mention is made of their young, though presumably they are born and raised as other otters are.

HISTORY: In 1722, a woman named Grace McGloighlin, nee Connolly, was killed by the dobhar-chú, and the details engraved on her tombstone. It is said that her husband, Terence came upon his wife's body and the sleeping creature and killed it, avenging her death and subsequently was pursued by the creature's mate across county Sligo. At the end of the chase, her husband is said to have killed the second dobhar-chú by lancing it at the base of its neck as it charged him. While there are accounts of sightings dated earlier than this, this is the most famous account.

Modern accounts continue to this day, including one in 2003 on Omey Island in Connemara, by an Irish artist and his wife, who were there camping. In the early hours of the morning there were woken by a strange yelping cry. When they investigated, the spied a creature as large as their Labrador swimming across the lake. It emerged and reared up on its hind legs to stand at least five foot tall before disappearing back into the water.

Similar creatures have been reported in Scotland, at Loch Gairloch and the Inner Hebrides Island of Skye as far back as 1510 and 1703, as well as a plethora of other water monsters.

There are other supersized otters known to exist, such as the South American giant otter (saro Pteronura brasiliensis), and the North Pacific sea otter (Enhydra lutris), but none lay claim to such lore and legend.

About the Artist

Although Jason Whitley has worn many creative hats, he is at heart a traditional illustrator and painter. With author James Chambers, Jason collaborates and illustrates the sometimes-prose, sometimes graphic novel, *The Midnight Hour,* which is being collected into one volume by eSpec Books. His and Scott Eckelaert's newspaper comic strip, Sea Urchins, has been collected into four volumes. Along with eSpec Books' Systema Paradoxa series, Jason is working on a crime noir graphic novel. His portrait of Charlotte Hawkins Brown is on display in the Charlotte Hawkins Brown Museum.

CAPTURE THE CRYPTIDS!

Cryptid Crate is a monthly subscription box filled with various cryptozoology and paranormal themed items to wear, display and collect. Expect a carefully curated box filled with creeptastic pieces from indie makers and artisans pertaining to bigfoot, sasquatch, UFOs, ghosts, and other cryptid and mysterious creatures (apparel, decor, media, etc).

http://CryptidCrate.com

Printed in the USA
CPSIA information can be obtained
at www.ICGtesting.com
CBHW021538240724
12124CB00006B/44